A SUMMER LIKE NO OTHER

(EM & NICK #1)

Elodie Nowodazkij

First Edition: July 2015
Second edition: September 2020

CHAPTER 1 - EM

The pop music blasts from the speakers so loudly that it resonates within me. I jump once, twice, three times with my fist in the air, and then my hips move to the pounding rhythm.

The mirrors on the wall aren't used to seeing me dance like this. I usually dance to Mozart, Tchaikovsky, Prokofiev, Minkus. Not to Madonna.

I tilt my head to the side. I don't want to rehearse the movements from any ballet choreographies, but I should. I rise on my toes into a *relevé*.

I don't want to be Emilia Moretti—sixteen-year-old ballerina who tries to perfect each single movement to the point of obsession. I lower my body down, bending my knees over my feet, into a *plié*.

I don't want to be the girl, who swears she doesn't care about being adopted but who has been trying to find her birth parents.

I stand on my toes again.

I don't want to dwell on the fact that I have the saddest crush on Nick—the best dancer at the School of Performing Arts and my brother's best friend.

I want to let go and dance.

I close my eyes and raise my hands, moving my lips and making up words as I sing off-key. I leap from the ground. My legs form a *grand jeté* that would have me thrown out of the School of Performing Arts: my front leg is not entirely straight, and I'm definitely not high enough in the air. But I don't care. I land on one foot, do little jumps and then turn and turn and turn—enjoying the moment, not worrying about anyone possibly watching me.

The summer has emptied the dorms and the hallways of the School of Performing Arts. And if my dad hadn't lost his job, I wouldn't be here either. I would be dipping my toes in the ocean, lying on the beach at the Hamptons, thinking of how to make Nick notice my new bikini. Those days of careless spending and adventures are gone.

My feet take me on another spin. I concentrate on the music, on the feeling of freedom that comes from letting my body move, on the possibilities ahead. Pushing away the thoughts that the music will end, that I will need to face reality, that this feeling of happiness will disappear.

"Nice, Em. But aren't you supposed to wear clothes when you're dancing?"

I gasp. Nick stands in the middle of the room. Shirtless. His sweatpants hang low like an Abercrombie model's. All strong biceps, ripped abs and chiseled torso.

Note to self: keep breathing.

"Wh-what are you doing here?" I stutter. My heart does its usual happy-to-see-you-Nick dance. Even though, ever since my father got fired, it's been a little tense between us. He's not supposed to be here. He's supposed to enjoy the beach where we used to have bonfires. He's supposed to dip in the water where we played Marco Polo. He's supposed to live the life we used to have. And of course, he's supposed to be tanning on the sand, flirting with every girl in a tiny bikini, breaking hearts.

"Hmmm...what could I be doing in the dance studio?" He raises an eyebrow in his aren't-you-cute-little-sister-of-Roberto way and I want to scream.

But I keep my voice as casual as possible. "Here, in New York." I roll my eyes. Not joining the usual group in the Hamptons may have sucked, but it was supposed to give me at least two months without seeing *him*.

"I was enjoying the show," he replies, laughing

"Yeah. Right." My cheeks flame as I stare into the deep green sea of regrets that is Nick's eyes.

He moves his hips to the music still blasting in the room. A room that is usually able to contain twenty students easily, but which now seems to be closing in on us. "I'm pretty sure this dance is not on the repertoire. But it should be. You looked great and like you were having fun."

"Fun," I blabber. He must be joking: I'm sweaty and out of breath, my hair is probably wild around my face, my posture is all wrong. But he doesn't glance away. His eyes roam my face, down my neck, up and down my body. My almost-naked body. I'm only wearing a bra and tiny shorts. Because I was supposed to be alone here and the stupid AC is being a real diva—working one second and then stopping for a minute while temperatures are hitting the hundreds. My hands curl around my middle, my ears feeling hotter than my own personal Hell.

"You never dance like this—like you're having the best time of your life." His gaze heats up. Or maybe it's me.

My top and my tights sit neatly folded on top of my gym bag. Right by the stereo. I shift on my feet, hesitating. Should I rush to get them? There's something about the way he looks at me that glues me to the floor.

He's looking at me like he sees me. Really *sees* me.

Maybe this is the wake-up call he needed to realize I'm not only Roberto's annoying little sister.

Get a grip, Em. Get a grip.

I clear my throat. "You still didn't answer my question. I thought you were supposed to be at the Hamptons with the rest of the gang." My voice falters but I keep my I-am-not-hurt mask. None of the friends I used to go to the Hamptons with returned my calls. I've received a grand total of one text in the past two weeks, telling me how much fun they're all having and that I'm missing out. Like I didn't know.

Nick crosses his arms over his chest. His very muscular arms. His very defined chest.

I really should get a grip. He's a dancer, he's got an amazing body because he's a dancer, because he puts in a lot of hours into training it, because that's his job. Other guys at the school have a perfect body too. But I don't drool over them, so why him?

He smiles and chuckles. "What's so funny?" I ask, blowing a strand of hair away from my face.

His chuckles turn into one of his happy-laughs, one of his laughs that usually would have me melting. Nick never laughs at me and right now, it almost seems he's trying to push me so I can forget about my bitterness. He winks. "You want to sound angry but you don't. You sound surprised...and maybe, do I dare say it? Happy to see me."

"Yeah, right. You're so full of yourself. Is that a requirement to be one of my brother's friends?" I stretch, grab the remote control lying on the floor and turn off the music. We do not need to have this conversation over the collection of eighties music I found in

Mom's closet. Something about listening to "Like a Virgin" right now seems...inadequate.

Or maybe too adequate.

"You know the only requirement to be one of your brother's friends is to like playing *Formula One* and *Mario Kart* and the occasional *Call of Duty*. Your brother is pretty easy to please. You, on the other hand, not so much."

"If my brother is so easy to please, why haven't you been to our place since school ended?" I stare at my shirt as if I could will it to fly to me, as if I developed supernatural powers in the last hour. Going to grab my shirt would mean brushing past him, and I'm not sure my heart could handle the proximity. "I've seen your brother. I kicked his ass at *Formula One* last night," Nick replies.

This time, my smile is real. Roberto hasn't said anything, but he missed hanging out with Nick. I know they only needed a bit of time to figure it out. "I guess I didn't get invited because you were afraid to lose." I can't help but sound a bit smug. I've got mad video-gaming skills.

"Or maybe because you're a sore loser." Nick grins the grin I love, the one that makes my heart beat faster than any ballet rehearsals or showcases.

And apparently, Nick cannot hear the thundering of my heart, cannot hear how it's beating so fast I'm afraid it's suddenly going to stop, cannot hear how it's dancing its own dance for him. Nope, instead of staying at a safe distance, he strides my way, so close I could almost touch him.

This is one of my dreams come true. Dreams. That must be it—I must be dreaming. Which means soon he's going to kiss me. He's going to whisper that he wants me, that's he's always wanted me, that he loves me. I lick my lips and take a deep breath.

But nope, instead of kissing me like he would in my dreams, he smiles one more time, steps away and walks to the bench on the other side of the room. He picks up my clothes, my gym bag and then brings them to me. "Come on, Em. My turn to rehearse."

My stomach clenches and I tilt my chin down.

Definitely not a dream.

And if it is a dream, it's a really shitty one

CHAPTER 2 - NICK

Em tucks a strand of hair behind her ear, again and again, her mouth slightly open and her chin tucked in—clear signs she's either angry or disappointed or both, but trying very hard to keep it all bottled up inside. The last time she looked like this was right after her father got fired. And my chest tightens, remembering how sad she was, how she couldn't even look at me for a few days.

But then, she squares her shoulders and stares right at me. My gaze drops to her lips. Lips that are so fucking inviting I should get a prize for not asking if I could kiss her. Only once. Only to taste those lips.

She snaps her fingers in front of me. "And why should I go?" she asks, putting a hand on her waist. "I was here first, Mister Entitlement."

And she's back, ladies and gentleman. I tilt my head to the side—going for the innocent, I'm-so-nice look. "I didn't know." That's a lie. Roberto told me where she was and yes, I had to rehearse, but I could have waited.

"But when you saw me dancing, you could have used another room. It's the best one, but it's not the only one." I can almost see her pump her fist in the air, because she thinks she found the solution—a way to prove me wrong. Her life mission, apparently.

"It is the only one open right now. They're remodeling the other ones." I pause. "I wasn't joking. You looked amazing." I've only seen her dance like this one other time. Like today, she was alone in a rehearsing room, and she completely lost herself to the move-ments. She's usually so put together, so serious about dancing, too much of a perfectionist to portray and communicate the emotions to the audience.

Her body was one with the music.

And she was hot.

She is hot. And...the wrong brain is taking over.

"Thanks," she replies, blushing and glancing everywhere but at me again.

I clear my throat, tempted to forget my promises to Roberto, tempted to forget I only do short-term relationships (ones with ex-piration dates), tempted to forget everything but her.

The crush I've had on her ever since she beat me at Mario Kart last year wearing shorts which showed her long legs has grown big-ger and bigger. Kind of like me now.

I shift around. "Anyways, there are rules." I sound like a dick. But there *are* rules I need to follow. Not the rules I'm talking to her about, but rules nonetheless. Strict rules. Not the ones her broth-er—my best friend—gave me, but my own.

Never fall for a girl. Never fall for *this* girl.

"And since when do you follow rules?" She stretches on her toes, goes back down, stretches back up—she's mesmerizing. And now I sound like an idiot.

She continues talking. "Apparently, since you decided the Hamptons weren't cool enough for you this year, we're going to have to share this room for the next few weeks. You can't come in here and tell me I'm done rehearsing simply because you said so."

"Did you sign your name on the sheet?"

"What sheet?" She stays on her toes and glances around the room.

"Online. There's a calendar of reservations for the rehearsal room, and it's been mine for the past twenty minutes. I was actually very generous to let you keep on dancing."

"Generous, my ass."

"Are we really having a discussion about your ass?" I tease her.

"You're impossible," she grunts, throwing her arm in the air and leaning against the mirror.

"There are rules about the mirror too."

"You're an asshole," she replies, but she stops leaning on the mirror. Emilia is known to follow the established rules, to try to be perfect. Her tone is angry but her lips are turned up in a half-smile, the one that says she thinks I'm funny. I love that smile.

"I see your mind is really set on that ass discussion," I answer, laughing. I can't help it. Em and I always have this easy banter, this kind of back and forth where we push each other's buttons but know the lines not to cross.

She sighs. "I give up. I didn't know about the sheet," she says.

"I'm glad I can teach you things. Oh, little one." I joke and expect her to get all pissy at me, but instead she steps toward me.

She's way too close.

She's not close enough.

"Little one? Really? Everyone knows size doesn't matter."

My mouth gapes open. "Did you say what I think you said?"

Her dimples deepen as she laughs. "You should have seen your face."

"What do you know about size anyways?"

She grunts. "Really. We're so not having this conversation either. I need a shower. I need to get back home. And I need you out of my face."

And I'm picturing her in the shower. I shift on my feet again; this is becoming very uncomfortable. "I'm here for the summer. And Roberto wants me to hang out. He told me I should come for dinner. Sooner than later."

"What?" Her eyes glance down and it seems she's trying to look upset, but instead there's almost hope on her face. Rob does want us to go back to the way things were before his dad got fired. But Rob has also warned me about flirting with Em. Rob has warned me to not break her heart.

I need to stop the flirting. Now. So, I lie. "Not tonight though. I have a date with Jen tonight."

"Jen—Jen?" She steps back and puts on her shirt in a hurry. "I can't believe you're going on a date with Jen. Again."

"Why not?" I shrug. She doesn't need to know that the only reason I dated Jen in the first place was because my dad told me to. The only reason I spent so much time with her was to help him land a business deal with Jen's parents.

"She was a total bitch to me." She stares at me like I've lost my mind.

"She sees you as a threat."

"Natalya is her t-threat. N-ot me," Emilia stutters. She only stutters when she's excited or hurt. I'm pretty sure she's not excited right now, and I have to hold myself back. I can't tell her that this date with Jen is not real. To tell the truth, I'm not even sure Jen is in the city. I should probably call her. She's not all that bad, and when we dated—for a whopping two weeks—she dropped the spoiled girl act, but Em and she have been rivals since they both got into the School of Performing Arts.

"You're a better dancer than you give yourself credit for," I tell her instead.

She shakes her head, pokes my chest. "I am an amazing dancer. But I know my place. I'm not the best dancer yet. I worry about my technique too much." She pauses. "Anyways, it's not about my dancing. It's about the fact that you're going out with Jen. She doesn't even like you."

My hand on my chest, I wince. "Hey, that hurts. Everyone likes me." Jen told me dating me was helping her social status at the school, so I didn't feel that bad about going out with her. She was using me, like I was using her.

"Every girl thinks you're hot. There's a difference." I must look hurt because Em frowns. "Fine, you're right. Everyone likes you."

I laugh. "I'm pretty likable. And glad to know you think I'm hot." I should stop this conversation right here and right now. "I have to rehearse, but I guess we'll see each other around."

"Pretty hard to avoid it."

It's getting pretty hard to avoid the...hardness down south too, but I can't let Em know about that. Em, who's totally off-limits. Em, who I can't stop thinking about. Em, who I know damn well I could hurt.

"See you around," I tell her and turn to the stereo on the side of the room. I hand her the Madonna CD, careful not to touch her fingers because I have only so much self-restraint.

She rushes out, grabbing her clothes and putting them on quickly before slamming the door behind her.

I close my eyes, breathing deeply.

Spending the entire summer with Em, dancing with Em, laughing with Em, talking with Em. Kissing Em. Caressing Em.

Both my heads seem to like that plan.

Fuck.

CHAPTER 3 – EM

The heat engulfs me. Even with an AC barely functioning, the building stayed somewhat cooler than the outside inferno. That or my entire body is in flames. There *was* a moment.

A moment like you see in movies, or read about in books.

I'm not sure if it was the way he was looking at me, the way he smiled when he first saw me, the way his voice turned much lower when he said I looked beautiful.

But it doesn't matter.

He's seeing Jen. Perfect Jen. Jen with her perfect skin and perfect smile and perfect ballet technique. Jen who feels entitled to everything, who does her best to sabotage me every chance she gets. Jen who fucking hates me. Ever since she dated Nick and he dumped her, she's hated me.

I enter Central Park instead of going straight into the subway, barely avoiding a group of tourists who are walking while taking pictures of everything.

I breathe in the sweet smell of cotton candy, a pang of regret and longing in my chest. Nick and I used to eat cotton candy in the Hamptons at least once every summer. It was something we did together, just the two of us, kind of an unspoken tradition.

I shake my head and stride through the crowds. Jen or no Jen. Moment or no moment. Nothing is going to change. He's got this weird bro code with Roberto that he can't date me, and he changes girlfriends as quickly as his *pas de deux*. And man, he can spin.

"Can you be careful where you're going?" a lady with a strong French accent hisses. She's holding two kids by the hands. One of them has an ice cream cone almost bigger than his face, and my bag swings dangerously close to it.

"I'm sorry." The words tumble out of my mouth and I hurry out of the way.

She mutters something I don't understand and then pulls her children with her.

My *La Vie en Rose* ringtone is almost too perfect for this moment. The woman turns around and actually smiles at me. One of those I'm-tired-and-sorry-I-was-bitchy smile. And the more I look at her, the more I see the lines underneath her eyes, the tears gathered in them, the way she keeps on looking behind her as if she's expecting someone else to be with her. But there's no one.

"Hi," I pick up.

"Hey sis, are you sleeping at the studio?" Roberto sounds amused.

"I'm on my way to Nonna's and then I'll head home. Where are you?"

"I'll be home soon," he replies, avoiding my question in true Roberto-fashion. And then he continues, "Did you run into Nick? He wanted to go rehearse too. He said something about a certain list you should be using."

My mouth gapes open. "You talked to Nick about my rehearsal?" I stop walking. "By the way, I didn't know you went to his place last night to play."

"It was about time." Roberto sighs. "It's not his fault Dad got fired."

My chest constricts remembering the look on Dad's face when he told us he no longer had a job. "I know."

Roberto clears his throat—his usual sign he doesn't want to get all sentimental. "Nick and I are planning on finding ways to have a blast since we're both stuck in hell for the summer. I'm sweating so much it's repulsive." He pauses. "The beach. That's more my scene. Anyways, wanted to let you know we're going to be moving some boxes in the pod tonight. Fun times."

"You know how to make everything fun," I reply.

"Be careful. See ya, sis." He hangs up and my eyes search for the woman with the two kids. They're by the Bethesda fountain. Nick and Roberto love that place because it's the starting point for Delta in Call of Duty: Modern Warfare 3. I have a love/hate relationship with the fountain because that's where I thought Nick was going to kiss me for the first time last winter. But instead of feeling his lips on mine, he kissed my cheek, cleared his throat and mumbled something about me being Roberto's little sister.

The kids splash each other, while the woman holds the cone, ice cream running down her fingers. She laughs once but then stops as if she shouldn't be laughing, as if the sound is all wrong.

"*On y va*," she tells her boys, who follow her without complaint, holding on to her like she's their lifesaver.

Before I can say anything—and really, what would I say?—she disappears into Central Park. We're the same height, have the same dark brown hair color, the same lost battle with our frizzy curls. And I have one of those sinking feelings that she could be my mother—or someone similar to my mother. She looked ready to collapse from sadness.

But at the same time, she seemed to be fighting for her kids' happiness.

Maybe that's what my mother did when she dropped me off at the hospital when I was only a newborn.

She was fighting.

MY MIND REELS DURING the entire ride to Brooklyn, where my grandmother Nonna lives. Between the encounter with the woman and knowing Nick was well aware I was in the studio, I'm equal parts excited and anxious about this summer, about seeing Nick, about looking for my birth parents. It could go wrong in so many ways, but maybe it will all work out, maybe it's going to be the best summer of my life. The train isn't as crowded as during the school year and I actually grab a seat—next to a woman about Mom's age who seems to be deep in her book.

To busy my hands, I pull out my cell from its designated spot in my bag—or as Roberto calls it, my OCD bag where everything has its place—and log into Facebook. Jen and I may not talk much, but we're "friends" on there. I click on her profile picture—the one where she's dancing a solo at last year's showcase—and scroll through her page.

She has a picture of the Eiffel Tower and then her status update says, "Paris was amazing. Loved shopping on the Champs, and visiting the Opera, but now time to get serious." She posted the link to the Lyon Opéra de Ballet. She did mention knowing someone over there.

She's posting pictures from France, she's been there for the past four days, she's checking out some dance companies in France.

Nick's such a liar. I'm not quite sure if I should laugh about it or be offended. After all, he made up going on a date with Jen to simply avoid spending more time with me—but then why did he come to the studio when he knew I'd be there?

"Asshole," I mutter and the lady next to me whispers, "Tell me about it."

We exchange a commiserating glance and then she gets back to her book. Something about being almost fifty and starting new again.

I'm not even seventeen yet, and I have the feeling I need to start all over again.

Note to heart: find someone else to have a crush on.

Note to self: stop talking to yourself, people might think you're weird.

I'm so deep in thought I almost miss my stop.

With my gym bag on my shoulder, I slide outside the metro and hurry up the stairs, turn right into the crowded street and take a deep breath when a breeze of air finally blows my way. The humidity and stuffiness of the last few days have almost been too much.

I miss the Hamptons.

In the Hamptons, I could sit on the sand, my legs in the water, enjoying the little wind by the sea.

In the Hamptons, it was all about bonfires, and laughter, and getting a tan, and time with Nick. Nick, who gave me his sweater when I was shivering one night on the beach. Nick, who always made sure I was having a good time. Nick, who makes it very hard to not fall for him.

But we had to sell the house we owned there. And when Dad told us about it, I managed to keep a smile on my face. There's no reason he should suffer even more knowing that we're disappointed. He's already so sad about everything.

Some new family is making new memories.

Good for them.

Nonna's restaurant is on the corner of the next block. I stop to clear my mind. Nonna can tell right away if I'm sad or worried or preoccupied. But my smile is genuine when I spot the big sign Nonna placed in front of her restaurant. "The Best Italian Food in New York—almost better than in Italy". She added a few tables outside, and one of the waiters is trying to convince a couple that they should experience Nonna's lasagna for themselves.

I slide past them and push the restaurant's door open. The AC blasts right in my face and I shiver.

"Hi Nonna," I call for my grandmother, who's been treating Brooklyn to her famous Italian dishes for the past forty years. I overhear her in the kitchen talking about some new dish she wants to make. And then she struts my way, her gray hair in a chignon, her black dress covered with a white apron. She's been wearing black ever since Poppa passed away two years ago.

"Hi, Bellissima," she replies and gives me a big hug. "I'm glad you're coming to see me."

"You know I always love to come here. Plus, no one is home yet. Dad is at work. Mom is at some charity event and Roberto is...somewhere either cramming for that research group he's part of this summer, or hanging out with some friends."

"Are you here to help me bake my famous baked Ziti, Bellissima?"

"I'd love to," I reply. "Let me wash my hands." The restaurant's not quite full yet, but the kitchen is already busy, preparing the main dish for the evening.

My Nonna hands me the onions. "Cut them like I taught you to."

And for the next thirty minutes, we cook in silence. It's one thing I love about being here with her. No questions, no judgment, no expectations except to be myself.

And for the thousandth time, I promise myself that no matter what I end up finding, no matter who my blood family is, no matter my feelings, I will never hurt my parents, Roberto or Nonna.

Never.

CHAPTER 4 - NICK

My steps were all wrong. My jumps weren't high enough, not fast enough, not good enough. My tempo majorly sucked. I rub the back of my neck.

This was one of the worst training sessions I've ever had. And I've had pretty bad ones in the past.

I need to get my shit together. Daddy Dearest is looking for any possible weaknesses, he's pushing me to stop thinking I can make a career out of dancing, he's threatening to pull the money plug. And it's too late to get a scholarship. So far, Mom's been on my side and Dad wants to avoid a scandal. But I need to do better.

I drop my bag in the hallway, already hearing my father telling me that it's not in its place. I almost bring it with me upstairs but then again, annoying my dad is half of the fun. The house is almost too cold, and I'm not sure if it's the fact the AC is set to sixty-five or because our family's been in a deep let's-pretend-everything-is-okay hole.

"You're home." Mom's in the kitchen pouring herself a glass of lemonade. Her hair is half-up, half-down, kind of crazy, compared to the very strict way she usually has it up. And she's wearing sweats for the first time in her life.

"What's up?" I ask and sit at the counter. She offers me a glass of lemonade which I take in my hands, still searching for any signs that she's either lost it, or maybe she's slugging back a cocktail a little earlier than usual.

"I'm going on vacation." She sips her lemonade, staring into space. "On spa-cation."

"Okay." I enunciate slowly, raising my eyes to the ceiling. Mom going to the spa is as new as me wanting to become a professional dancer.

Mom places a hand over mine. And I almost jolt back. That's new. Personal contact in this house isn't the norm. Mom air-kisses her friends, she gives me the occasional hug (the birthday hug, the Christmas hug, the celebratory-in-front-of-everyone hug after a show). She never touches my hand like she's doing right now—like she wants to pass on some sort of message to me, which I don't understand.

"It might be a long spa-cation. I need some distance," she says and bites her lip. "Not from you. Never from you. You know that, right?"

"I'm pretty hard to be away from," I joke because I have no clue what else to do in this situation, and it's easier than to dwell on the reasons she wants to leave. Mom and Dad have been fighting a lot. Even more than usual.

She removes her hand and her bland smile is back on. "True. Anyways. Be good while I'm gone." She doesn't tell me to listen to my father. Interesting.

"Always. I'm the definition of good." Good at school. Good at dancing. Good in bed. Hmm, not something Mom probably wants to hear.

"I have to pack. I'm going to the same place as always. Come visit me?" Her tone is all over the place between sad and excited, as if she's not sure what emotion she should convey.

"Of course, I will."

"I'm leaving in an hour."

That means if I didn't come home now, I probably wouldn't have seen her. I would have gotten one of her handwritten notes on my desk that may have said more about the reasons behind her spacation.

She's more truthful on paper.

CHAPTER 5 - EM

Nonna pulls her cannoli recipe in front of me. It's full of scribbles and marks, like "Did this recipe to celebrate our twenty-year anniversary. Needed more sugar."

She sets the ingredients on the table in the far right corner of the kitchen, where the service is slowing down. "Come on, Bellissima. I'm thinking of serving those during coffee time tomorrow." She kisses my cheek. "Call me if you need help, or can't read my handwriting." She goes back inside the restaurant, where she always makes a point to talk to every single family, to every single customer.

My hands are deep in yummy, creamy dough when Mom waltzes into the kitchen in her favorite cocktail dress, the one she says reminds her of Grace Kelly: elegant but understated in its elegance. It's perfect for her: it highlights her blue eyes, and she does look like a movie star with the way the navy sequin dress floats at the bottom.

"I didn't know you were coming in," I tell her after she kisses my forehead, not caring I might be getting flour on her clothes.

"I thought you'd like to share the driver with me, instead of taking the metro."

"The driver?" My voice rises and I clear my throat.

"Don't look so worried. I'm not crazy. The other organizers of the gala decided I needed a driver to go back home, and I decided I'd share the comfort with you."

I go along with the pretend-game and smile too. "Great! It's so humid my hair is scary frizzy."

"Did you convince all those important people to give money?" Nonna asks when she steps into the kitchen again, and then continues without waiting for an answer. "Did you mention the restaurant to them? I can picture them eating my pesto and realizing they've never had something so good." Nonna laughs.

"I did mention the restaurant to a few people," Mom says, taking a bite of the pastry Nonna's handing to her.

"So the event went well?" I roll the dough one last time before washing my hands.

"Good, good...the event was good." She sighs and bites her lip again, but then she must see me staring at her teeth because she laughs. "It's all fine. It's the last charity event I was organizing and then, we almost have a buyer for the house in Manhattan. It's going to be fine. By September, we'll be living next door from here, and we'll get to eat at Nonna's every single day." She gives me a hug and I squeeze her back. "How was your practice?"

"Nick was there—apparently I have to register for the room online over the summer. I didn't think I needed to book anything, but whatever."

Mom chews her lip again. "I'm so happy Nick and Roberto are back to normal. Roberto told me they hung out at Nick's house last night." Mom's smile turns brighter and more real. "And I'm glad you're not holding a grudge against him. I really hope you kids don't suffer from what's going on. This has nothing to do with you." She pauses. "Nick should come to dinner soon."

Nonna jumps into the conversation, clapping her hands. "Yes, yes. Nicholas should come to dinner. I'll make him lasagna, he loves my lasagna," she says. "You used to think Nick was cute, no?" And as always, Nonna doesn't have a filter when it comes to my private life. I kiss her cheek.

"He's okay," I reply, desperately wanting to change the subject.

"I'm glad he decided to stay in the city. You and your brother can use a friend. And Nick is a real friend. I'm sorry again we didn't go to the Hamptons this year." Mom gives my shoulder a squeeze.

"It's fine. I need to practice anyways," I reply. It's on the tip of my tongue to mention the search for my birth parents. I've talked to them about it before, but I don't want to bring it up now. Some days, Mom seems fine with my quest, supporting me, answering my questions. Other days, she seems worried, like she's losing a part of me.

"We should get going. The driver is waiting and we have so much to pack and move tonight." She winks at me. "Maybe I should ask Roberto if Nick can help us with moving some of the boxes downstairs."

"You wouldn't." I croak, drying my hands over and over again.

"We do need help." Mom chuckles.

Nonna's happy wrinkles around her dark eyes deepen as she laughs loudly. "My Dino is lucky to have married you, Amanda."

"I'm lucky to have married him," she replies and kisses Nonna on the cheek too. Mom may look way different than Nonna with her reddish hair and blueish eyes, but she fits right into Dad's family. They were proud of their son for "making it" as they used to say, for being a fancy Wall Street guy, but when Dad lost his job, Nonna was here for him.

She helped us secure the place next door to the restaurant and helped Dad find a new job. It's not as prestigious and we definitely can't keep the same lifestyle we used to, but at least it's going to pay the bills and pay for school.

Mom wraps an arm around my shoulder as we step out into the humidity that is New York in the summer. "If you really don't want Nick to come tonight, I won't call him. But you can't avoid people who make you feel alive," Mom says.

"He's a player. And I'm not interested," I reply, glancing everywhere and anywhere but not looking Mom in the eyes. An extra pair of hands would help tonight. It's funny how friends disappear at the same time money runs out. The driver opens the doors for us and I sink into the leather seats, breathing the brand new car smell that always comes with these type of rides, enjoying the air-conditioning and the way the windows are tinted so no one can see us.

I turn to Mom, who's sipping from a bottle of water. "Actually, I'm sure Roberto would love to have Nick for dinner. Let me call him." My heart skips a beat—calling Nick is usually not that nerve-wracking. "I have something to ask him too," I say, thinking about Jen, and his blatant lies about going out with her this evening.

His voice mail picks up and my stomach warms at his deep voice. "Hi, you've reached Nick. You know what to do at the beep."

"Hey Nick, it's Em. Would you happen to be free for dinner tonight? We could use some help with the move. I know you mentioned something about Jen but unless she's jet-setting back from France, she might be late for your date."

CHAPTER 6 - NICK

I listen to Em's voice mail at least three times before texting her back that I'll come over and help. Her voice in the message sounds amused, but also a bit disappointed. And why the hell am I analyzing her voice mail? This is ridiculous.

I haven't been to Em's and Rob's house in over a month, but I could still get there with my eyes closed. After all, I used to spend almost every evening with them, soaking in the family fun, before getting into the School of Performing Arts. I walk with my head high, nodding at the doormen I recognize like I don't have a care in the world, but I'm rehearsing what I will say to Dino—their dad—if I see him. "I'm sorry about my father" or "I had no idea he was going to fire you. I promise."

I'm so deep in thought I almost run into a gorgeous girl pushing a little boy.

"Sorry," I mutter.

And she smiles. "It's okay." She's got an accent. German, maybe? She must be a nanny—she's with two other girls, and they continue their conversation as I walk past them. They're bitching about the families they're working for.

My nanny probably did the same while I was growing up. She probably told all the other nannies how awful I was. According to the psychologist we all saw as a family, I was only trying to get attention.

Maybe I should tell those nannies that the moment will pass. Kids only try to get attention from one source for so long before they get their fix somewhere else. My chosen method is pretty healthy: no drugs, no drinking...only all eyes on me while I dance. And girls.

Girls, girls, girls.

Actually, Nanny One is pretty hot, especially with the accent. She has short light brown hair, and her big boobs are almost spilling out of her blouse.

She must feel me staring at her, because she turns around. But before I can work the charm I notice Em carrying a box into a moving truck, all by herself. The box is almost bigger than her and her face contorts under the effort. She's going to trip and hurt herself. If she hurts herself, she won't be able to dance. If she can't dance, she's going to be depressed. If she can't dance, I won't see her as often and I'll be miserable.

"Are you trying to prove something to someone?" I ask her as I relieve her of the heavy box.

She breathes heavily. "Are you trying to get it on with Katrin because Jen is out of town?"

"Katrin?" I slide the box on top of another one and turn back to her.

She points to the girls I was admiring a few seconds ago. "The nanny you were about to hit on."

"Katrin. Is she American or...?" I waggle my eyebrows.

"She's German." She raises one finger at a time as she enunciates the rest super slowly. "She's here for the summer. She loves going to Central Park and she doesn't understand why she has to work fifteen hours a day while the mom is a stay-at-home mom. Oh, and she likes girls. So, nice try."

"Did she hit on you? Oh please, tell me she did. I am getting the best girl-on-girl images in my mind. You. That girl, Katrin. A ballet studio. With all the mirrors. A kiss. Or two. Or more..."

She punches my shoulder. "You're so dumb. No, she didn't hit on me, I met her at Starbucks the other day and we started talking."

"You're talking to people now, not just hitting them?"

"And you're losing your mojo. First, Jen who escapes to France before your hot date, and then you almost hit on poor Katrin, who doesn't want anything to do with you."

She's kidding me. Me, losing my mojo? I don't think so. I stare at Em, at her long legs, her full lips, and I gently tuck a strand of her wild brown hair behind her ear, my finger slowly caressing her cheek.

She sucks in a breath and I bend down, until my lips are at her ears. "Do you want to test that theory?"

"What theory?" She doesn't move, and I'm not even sure she breathes. My entire body reacts to hers, and I can't remember what I wanted to prove. I'm under her spell.

"Hey bro!" Roberto yells from the stairs. "Thanks for coming!"

Em retreats at her brother's voice, muttering something I can't hear, but the slouch of her shoulders is a tell that she's disappointed. My hand automatically reaches for hers, wanting to comfort her, maybe even wanting to see if she'll take the risk of her brother seeing us, wanting to test myself too. It's nothing but a brief touch, a brief brush of our fingers, a brief hurricane of feelings. Our eyes lock. Hers are darker than usual, full of questions and desire.

For once I'm tempted not to move. For once, I'm tempted to check if maybe Rob changed his mind, if maybe he would give me the benefit of the doubt, or maybe he would realize his little sister is big enough to make her own decisions

"Thanks for coming!" Rob's almost by our side and Em lets go of my hand, stepping further away from me.

"Em!" I call and she turns to me. Her lips are slightly parted as if she's ready for a kiss, but instead she gives me the finger and laughs as if it was all a big joke.

Rob slaps me on the back, maybe a bit harder than necessary. He eyes me carefully. "Is everything okay?" It's funny how even though they don't share the same DNA, they do the same frown with their eyebrows when they think I'm getting myself in trouble.

"The usual," I reply. Me lusting after Em is not new, so technically it's not a lie.

"If you say so," he says slowly, raising an eyebrow. He glances between Em and me. "We've got a lot of work to do. Mom says we have to earn our dinner tonight by moving the boxes from the living room."

"Let's do this," I answer and follow him inside without looking at Em.

Roberto's my best friend. He's the one who jumped in front of me when four guys in middle school pounded on me with their fists, kicking me in the stomach and spitting on me. He's the one who helped me fight them off, telling them to "shut up" when they called me names: "fag, dick sucker, sissy." They thought I was gay because I was a dancer. When they disappeared at the corner of a street, Rob—the popular school wrestler, the guy who loved math and football, the guy who got asked to the school dance by five girls—turned to me and blurted, "I think I'm gay."

I replied, "I really like girls." And we both laughed.

We've been as close as brothers ever since.

I can't fuck that up, but I can't stop thinking about Emilia.

CHAPTER 7 – EM

Of course, Roberto had to kill the moment. I'm pretty sure Nick was about to kiss my neck. My body warms to new highs that have nothing to do with the hot weather as I think about his lips touching me.

"Thank you so much for coming over to help," Mom says right as Dad enters the house, dropping his briefcase a little loudly.

"This job is a joke," he says and pales when he sees Nick, sitting at the table.

"We were waiting for you for dinner." Mom stands up and gives Dad a kiss on the lips, leaning in to whisper something in his ear. He nods but his posture is still stiff, and he doesn't even loosen his tie.

I bring the dish of spaghetti carbonara to the table and serve everyone before taking my usual spot—next to Nick. *Hello, torture.*

"Em told me you also went to rehearse today." Mom's voice is almost too enthusiastic, but at least she's making an attempt at conversation.

"I did. But I was distracted," Nick replies, and did I see him glancing at me?

"Why did you decide to stay here this summer?" Mom asks, and Roberto mutters something about Nick not needing to answer.

"Dad wants me to help a bit in the office this summer." Nick doesn't look down, he doesn't avoid the answer in front of my father.

Dad's fork falls on his plate and he clears his throat. "How is your father doing?"

"Good, thank you," Nick says. And then shovels another spoonful of spaghetti in his mouth. The dining room is almost empty of all decorations: the walls are bare except for one picture of Nick's dad and mine together in front of some gala.

"He hasn't called me back."

"Dino." Mom's tone is gentle, but she narrows her eyes into *the* look—the one that usually shuts my father up in less than a second. She doesn't use that look a lot, but it's effective, and Dad even jokes about it sometimes.

Dad shakes his head and barks a laugh. "What? I'm supposed to shut up?" His voice rises and I've never heard him like that—so bitter. "I'm supposed to say nothing while my best friend screwed me over? I'm supposed to have his son over for dinner like nothing ever happened?" He pounds his fist on the table. "Bullshit!"

Roberto hisses, "No matter what happened, is it Nick's fault?" He leans forward on the table. "Dad, I asked you a question: is it Nick's fault?"

Nick shifts on his seat. "I should go. I'm sorry. I should go."

Mom shakes her head. "No. Don't go." She turns to Dad. "Dino, Rob asked you a question. And I think you know the answer."

Dad stares into his plate of spaghetti. We used to have elaborate meals, we used to have a chef coming once a week for a tasting of some sort. We used to have a maid, we used to be rich, but I never thought being rich was something that defined us, defined who we are.

Dad clears his throat and leans back in his chair. "Nick, please stay." Dad looks up. "I'm sorry. Amanda's right—this has nothing to do with you."

Nick's eyes widen and I'm tempted to sneak my hand underneath the table to offer some support, to let him know that I'm here. "I'm so sorry. My father is..."

"Charles is a businessman, and he did what was needed for his business."

"But you're his friend."

"Business and friendship don't mix. Don't worry, we'll have cigars again soon, once I'm back on my feet. And you're always welcome here. You are Roberto's best friend and you're always there for Em. We appreciate that."

For the first time, the lines around Dad's eyes appear more pronounced. His hand shakes a little as he brings the Diet Coke to his parched lips. His shoulders are slouched; he used to always stand tall. Mom covers his other hand with hers and smiles their special smile. It's the one she usually has for him when he doesn't look, when he helps Roberto with his homework, when he hugs his mom, or when he makes her laugh after a hard day.

My heart warms because no matter what, my mom and dad are here for one another.

And again, I'm tempted to show Nick I'm here for him too.

But Roberto beats me to the punch. "Hey Nico, do you want to go hang out at your place again tonight?"

Nick shifts on his seat. "How about we go to the pinball place tonight? I heard they got the new Avengers pinball!"

Roberto smiles. "You know I rock at pinball. Remember, two years ago in the Hamptons, I kicked your ass."

"Actually, Em kicked both of our records that night," Nick says but doesn't look at me.

Roberto nods. "Let's do it then. You and I. Old-school pinball machines. I'm supposed to meet someone later, but I can postpone.

Come on, last night I kicked your ass—maybe tonight you'll get lucky." No one bothers asking me what I want to do. And I can't help feeling a bit left out. When we lost everything, I also lost my so-called friends. Dancing and Nonna's restaurant are my world now.

Maybe I could go back to the studio later and rehearse, or maybe I could see Nonna again and ask if she could finally share the secret to her tiramisu. Learning how to create dishes, how to recreate them, is relaxing. In the restaurant, no one expects me to fail. *I* don't expect myself to fail.

Nick gently nudges me. "Do you want to join us?"

Roberto smiles. "That's a great idea. I love how she beats you every single time."

I want to go.

But instead of saying yes, I shrug. "Nah. I'll pass this time. I might go dance again tonight. I'm pretty sure no one requested the studio at eight p.m."

"Tomorrow, if you want, we could work on the choreography from the last showcase together."

My heart beats so fast I'm sure everyone at the table hears it. "Sure. That sounds good," I reply.

"Tomorrow at five?"

"Five it is," I answer.

Note to self: don't be too full of hope.

CHAPTER 8 - NICK

Modern Pinball is crowded as always. But we don't have to wait long to get two machines side by side. This place is super clean—not like Video Games Forever, the arcade we sometimes go to which smells like old food and old cigarettes. Rob's playing on the Avengers machine while I'm starting on the Mustang one. It's nice to hang out together again. Yesterday was the first time since my father fired his that he came over to my place. It was awkward at the beginning, but after he beat me at Formula One, he turned to me and said: "Your dad and mine can figure their shit out. It's not our business. And it's none of their business that we're best friends."

That settled it.

"You suck even more tonight!" Rob says and then clears his throat. "Was everything okay when I came outside earlier? You and Em seemed pretty intense."

"Everything was fine," I reply, my throat dry.

"She's not mad at you. She's upset about moving, about Dad losing his job and she's super focused on dancing and finding her birth parents."

I hold my hand up. "We're fine. Last summer, when we talked about her birth parents, she said she wanted to wait until she was eighteen to find them. What happened?"

"She's been more and more restless about it. I've told her she needed to wait, but you know her, the more you tell her she shouldn't do something, the more she wants to do it."

"But it's about her birth parents; I'm sure it's not about her being stubborn." I crack my knuckles after winning a bonus round.

"I don't want to see her hurt," Rob says.

"I don't either," I whisper, but Rob doesn't hear me—instead his eyes glance at a point behind me.

"I told you I had plans, right? Well, my plans have arrived and I really want you to meet him," he says and for the first time since I've known him, his voice quivers and he seems unsure of himself. Nervous.

"Mysterious guy?" I ask, teasing him.

"Serious guy," Roberto replies and stands up. He gives the newcomer a hug. The guy looks different than Roberto's usual flings. He's tall and dark-haired with dark eyes, which is Rob's style, but he's more than that. One, he's not all-muscle: he's rather lean and he's got glasses. Two, he's holding a messenger bag with books inside of it and not a fitness magazine, and three, he actually knows how to smile.

"Nick, this is my friend—Giovanni."

"Nice meeting you." Giovanni has a super heavy Italian accent. "Roberto talks so much about you."

"He probably told you he's better than me at all things video games." I lean in. "But I let him win, that's why."

Rob smiles. "Giovanni is Italian, he's here from Milano and he's studying astrophysics with me." He speaks much faster than usual and he fidgets. Rob never fidgets. "Well, not with me. He's in the astrophysics program, I'm in the nanophysics program. But it's the same building."

"Cool," I tell Giovanni and shake his hand.

"We have to go. I'm walking Giovanni back to his apartment and we need to study, but I wanted you to meet him," Rob says and stands up. "I have been kicking your ass since we got here. Probably because you've had your mind somewhere else. And for some reason, I have a feeling this somewhere else includes my sister." He pauses and his happy-careless smile morphs into a frown. "We've talked about that, dude."

"And you usually never say dude...I guess things can change."

"Unless you can promise my sister more than a fling then, nope, nothing can change." His hands land on both my shoulders. "You understand, right?"

I have no choice but to look him in the eyes as I reply. "I understand."

It's a lie.

"WHERE ARE YOU?" MY dad's voice carries through the entire ground floor. After coming home from Modern Pinball, I've been chilling in the living room, watching TV on the super comfy leather couch, kind of waiting for Dad to come back from his cocktail party. But I must have fallen asleep.

"You left for the spa without telling me? What is wrong with you, Annie?" He's talking to Mom, or rather yelling at Mom. I get up and follow the sound of his voice. The door of his office is open and he's sitting at his desk, a whiskey in his hand.

"You really think that's the answer! That you leaving is the answer! Goddamn it, we are married for better and worse. Not only for when it suits your fucking highness!" He pauses. "No, I will not apologize. And stop it, stop telling me it's all my fault. I was trying to do the right thing! I didn't know until last month..." He takes a sip of his drink. "I have no idea if Amanda knows or not."

What does Em's mom have to do with any of this?

Dad leans back on his chair. "It's not like we had a drink and talked about what happened sixteen years ago!" He downs the rest of his whiskey in one shot and flips through a file on his desk. "Of course, Emilia's adoption is legal. Claire Carter has nothing to say. Do not dare contact her. And we need to speak before you hire a fucking divorce lawyer." He slams his fist on the desk. "Do not dare throw our marriage in the trash without talking to me first!"

It's not the first time my parents have talked about getting a divorce and it probably won't be the last, but...Em's adoption, I've never heard a word about it from them.

I mold my back to the wall.

I could go in and face my dad, but I've learned the hard way that he will not budge if he doesn't want to.

I need to go upstairs before he sees me.

I need to step away from here.

I need to talk to Emilia.

CHAPTER 9 – EM

Our family used to go to brunch quite often, especially on weekends, but today, we're all sitting at the table, talking about the move, the restaurant, Nonna, my dancing, Roberto's research, Mom's last fundraiser. Trying to sound normal and cheery and happy. And failing.

I clear my throat. "I've received a notification on Facebook that someone might have more information about my birth parents."

Everyone turns to me: Mom's hands shake, Roberto frowns and Dad's eyes widen.

"What are you talking about?" Dad says and turns to Mom. "What is she talking about?"

I hate when he speaks as if I'm not in the room. "She's right here." I point to my face. "And I'm talking about the Find My Birth Parents group. I showed it to you last week."

"I thought we agreed you would wait until you're eighteen."

"No. That's not what we agreed. We agreed I could start searching, but that I needed to keep you updated on my progress. Mom said she would help."

"That's true." Mom's voice trembles and Roberto glares at me.

Dad takes a deep breath and closes the conversation with his usual, "We'll talk about this later."

I PLOP MYSELF ON MY bed, lie down with my eyes open, thinking about what I could have said differently to convince them. Maybe if I didn't snap at them, maybe if I told them again that it didn't change the way I feel about them, maybe if I told them I have the feeling I'm losing myself not knowing where I come from.

Three fast taps and one slow tap on my door snap me away from me feeling sorry about myself. It's Roberto's and my secret knock, the one we came up with when we were younger and grounded and defying the rules.

"What do you want?" I call.

"Can I come in?" he asks, and his voice sounds way too serious. With the way he was looking at me during dinner, I know he's not about to tell me that I'm right and Dad's wrong. But I also can't leave him in the hallway after he's used our secret knock.

"Whatever," I reply and hide my face under my arm.

The door screeches open and he clears his throat three times. "I don't understand," he says and nudges me. "Don't be a baby, look at me."

"According to you, I'm the baby of the family anyways," I whine. I hate it but I can't help it. From time to time, I revert to my twelve-year-old self—insecure and whiny. When Roberto was fourteen and pushing my buttons.

"You're acting like one." He sighs. "Come on Em, let's talk about this." He pauses. "Rationally."

"Because of course I'm not being rational. Of course, there's something wrong with me for wanting to meet my parents. Of course there's something wrong." I look up at him.

"And in one second, you go from baby to drama queen," he says. I would be offended if he didn't smile the way he does. It's his half smile, the one he only has when he gets hurt and doesn't want to show it. Roberto never wants to show he has feelings.

"What do you want to tell me?" I sit up and pat the spot next to me. Instead of sitting there, he pulls a chair over and sits in front of me, boring his eyes into mine.

"I'm afraid you're going to get hurt," he says.

"But isn't that supposed to be my decision?"

"Wasn't that supposed to be your birth parents' decision?" He pauses. "Listen, they abandoned you outside this hospital for a reason. They may not want to be found. And let's say you do find them; what are you going to do?"

I glance at my nails...they're still pinkish from the last nail polish I used. I don't chew my nails, but I have a very big urge to check my hair for split ends. I run my hair through my fingers, and Roberto gently slaps them away.

"I'm not saying it's easy for you. But I don't want it to become even more difficult. What do you want to find? Why are you even doing this?"

"Because I don't know who I am. I'm afraid of what I could find, but I'm even more afraid of not finding anything. I'm afraid that a part of me will always wonder, always worry."

"And if you find them and they're fucked up or they hurt you. Do you want a relationship with them? They kicked you to the curb!"

"We don't know that for sure! I was wrapped in a baby blanket. Lovingly. Someone did love me." I look away from him, hating my voice for breaking, hating myself for breaking along with it. I wipe away my tears and blink super fast to avoid any new ones. "Why can't you be supportive?"

"Sometimes, it feels like you're not happy with what you got. That you want a redo." Roberto stands up. "We're your family."

"And I'm happy for that. Nothing will change the fact that you're my brother."

"I hope you're right. Because right now, it feels like it has already changed things."

"It hasn't," I protest but still can't look at him. The tension I feel is mounting. Because of the search he doesn't approve of. Because he doesn't understand me.

"You don't have to do it alone," Roberto says. And I know he wants me to ask him for help. But I can't. Not right now. I don't want to add any additional pain to the one he's clearly already feeling.

"I know," I reply. "Thank you," I add. And he nods one time before leaving my room. I stretch my muscles and slowly get up where my laptop's standing.

And I lose myself in the search.

CHAPTER 10 - NICK

What's the best way to tell Em? Do I even tell her? What do I fucking know? Not much...but she's looking for her birth parents, she's set on the idea of meeting them, she's hopeful. My fingers dialed her number five times, but every time I stopped myself. Telling her on the phone seemed wrong.

I hurry up the stairs, down the hallway, push open the door to the studio.

And my mind goes blank. Em's already there, but she's not dancing. Instead she's lying on the floor with her eyes closed.

"That's not the place to take a nap. If Svetlana could see you, she would rip you a new one," I tell her, and can't help but chuckle. Svetlana is one of our nicest teachers, but sleeping in her class would still be a criminal offence.

"I'm not sleeping. I'm visualizing," Em replies, still with her eyes closed. "Nata does this every single time we have an audition or something important to rehearse for, and she's the best dancer at school. Better than any seniors, better than anyone, really."

"She's not better than me," I joke, even though Natalya—Emilia's roommate—is a wonderful dancer. Em smiles. I want to see her smile more often. I rub the back of my neck, wondering if I should tell her or wait until I have more answers.

"It's a close call," she answers. "But the thing is? What I'm sure of is that I'm trailing behind."

I focus on her, on the moment. "You're an amazing dancer."

"Who has the technique but can't let go. When I'm on stage, I can't let myself simply be. I can't be me. Because I have no idea who I am." She finally opens her eyes and turns to rest on her left elbow. I swear I'm not appreciating how that position makes her boobs look bigger. She continues, "You know who you are. You were always so sure about who you were. You never let anyone tell you what to do, what to believe in. It's like you know so much better than the rest of us who you truly are, and you're not afraid to show it."

Her lips turn into a smile that crushes my chest—it's sadder than any choreography I've ever danced, and I danced the role of Hilarion in *Giselle,* dying at every performance for two months. "I know how to pretend," I tell her. "Is that why you want to find your real parents?" I bore my eyes into her, trying to figure out if that's really what she wants, or if it's what she thinks she should do.

"My *real* parents are the ones who have been raising me, they're the ones who have to tell me to loosen up, they're the ones who were there for me when I had to get my appendix removed, the ones who taught me to walk, to talk..." She stares behind me. Her voice falters. "But a part of me always wonders." Her eyes gaze into mine and she whispers, "Before getting into the School, do you remember the physical we had to take?"

I nod. "Of course."

"Those questions about hereditary diseases, and about father, mother, siblings and all that, I couldn't answer them." The words rush out of her mouth now, like she's been holding them in for such a long time. "And then that one time Mom was late picking me up, I thought maybe they decided they didn't want me anymore. Another time, we were on holidays and this woman came and stared at me. I thought maybe she recognized me, maybe she gave birth to me. Sometimes, I can't look at strangers without wondering." She sighs. "I'm a mess."

"Everybody is." I stand up over her and extend my hand. I know how to distract her, if only for a few minutes. Then, we can talk. Then, I can spill my guts. Then, we can analyze everything. But right now, I only want to erase her worries. "Come on, let's dance. I want you to do something though."

"What?"

"Let me lead and close your eyes, let your body do the talking, lose yourself in the moment."

She nods, uncertain, and takes my hand. I wrap an arm around her waist and without any music on, I lead her into an arabesque. My fingers guide her as they trail down the side of her body.

We move together. As one. Our bodies are in a harmony you can't fake; the chemistry between us is off the roof. Her movements are fluid and real.

When we stop, I'm almost out of breath and her laugh is my new favorite music. She looks up at me, still in my arms and if I bend down only slightly, I'll finally taste her lips.

And I will.

I can't help myself.

But then she surprises me: she rises on her toes and whispers, "You're the best." And then her lips mold themselves to mine. Tentative at first, but then bolder.

I can't get enough. I can't break away. I can't for the life of me remember why this is a bad idea.

I open her mouth to my tongue and press her even closer. One of my hands stays on the small of her back, while the other cups her face.

She's so sweet and passionate.

She's everything.

CHAPTER 11- EM

I can't get enough of him, of the way his arms tighten around me before one of his hands caresses my cheek, of the way he's kissing like it's inevitable, impossible to resist, incredible, of the way his lips trail down my neck while he whispers my name.

I never want it to end.

I know it needs to stop, otherwise I'm not sure my heart will ever recover.

I slowly pull away and then take his hand in mind. "Thumb war?" I ask and he laughs.

"Thumb war," he replies. It used to be my way of helping him when his parents fought all the time or when he had a bad grade at school, or when he thought his dad would never let him dance.

His eyes smile almost as much as his lips, and the butterflies in my stomach are not only flapping their wings, they're doing pirouettes after pirouettes.

Our thumbs intertwine and we spend the next ten minutes laughing, talking about everything but that sizzling kiss.

"You have no idea how much I want to kiss you again," he says out of nowhere.

"I kissed you," I reply, tilting my head. "Technically, I was the kisser and you, my friend, were the kiss-ee."

"You have a point," he replies and then rubs the back of his neck. My stomach drops to my ankles because that's his tell he's about to do something he doesn't like, something he feels obliged to do. I don't want to hear him tell me what it is. I don't want to hear him tell me that we shouldn't kiss again, so I say it first.

"I wanted to see what all the fuss was about. And I mean, I get it, but it was not grandiose. Nothing to lose my sleep over."

He furrows his eyebrows. "So this kiss meant nothing, right?"

"Nope. Nothing at all." I lean back on the cold studio's floor again. "One way to distract myself."

"I was your distraction?"

"Hurts, no? Imagine all the girls you said that to before; they probably didn't want to only be your flavor of the hour."

"I have an understanding with them—they know what they're getting into," he says and sits next to me. "What was I distracting you from?"

I bite the inside of my cheek and raise my arms above my head, relaxing my body completely, my lips still tingling from our kiss. I turn my head to look at him. He knows almost everything about me, and he's always been there for me: he showed me the ropes when I first got into the School, he covered for me the one time I got drunk at a party and made sure I got home okay, he spent hours rehearsing with me when I asked him to, and even when I didn't. He doesn't say a word, waits for me to be ready to talk again. "I told you. It's hard to see people in the streets, at the movies, in Central Park and wonder... Sometimes, I wonder if they're even still alive, what their stories were, why they left me like this. I could have died, I could have stopped breathing and they wouldn't have known. Why didn't they want me?" I pause. "And I love my family. I do. I don't want any other one, but am I enough for them? Roberto could be on his way to win a Nobel Prize in Physics—he makes them proud. I can't even make it to the top of my class. And part of me thinks it's because I can never clear my mind of all the questions

I have. I can never let go, because I don't know what I'm supposed to let go of."

He clears his throat, shifts next to me. I sit up and our arms touch. They're aligned. He clears his throat again—I've never heard him this nervous. I tilt my head. "What's wrong?"

"What if I could help you?"

"What?" I stand up so fast my head gets as dizzy as if I didn't use an anchor point for a pirouette.

"What if I could help you find your mom?" Nick asks, rubbing the back of his neck and then glancing at the door. "What if I told you that my father knows something?"

"What do you mean?"

"I overheard my father arguing with my mom last night. He was yelling at her, and telling her not to leave him."

My heart aches for him, at the way his voice turns all robotic as it does when he tries to protect himself. But before I can say anything, he continues. "He said something about your adoption, about your mom not knowing about whatever it is he's hiding and telling my mom not to contact Claire Carter."

My body shifts back and my heart hammers. "Wh-what are you saying?" I shake my head without saying another word. Claire Carter? That's not possible—it doesn't make any sense.

"That's what he said. And I tried to find more information yesterday, but I couldn't. The name sounds familiar." His voice turns into a noisy background. Claire Carter—I remember that name. It's fuzzy, but I remember it. I've only seen her once years ago at one of Dad's and Nick's Dad's office parties. I remember Mom laughing with her at the party. I was maybe eight. Mom told her she talked to her more than she talked to Dad because he was always busy in meetings.

She was Dad's assistant.

CHAPTER 12 – NICK

I'd like to punch past-me in the face.

For several reasons.

One, present-me can't take enough cold showers. If I ever thought that one make-out session with Em would be sufficient, I was delusional.

Two, past-me should have never let her leave the studio after telling her about Claire Carter. She muttered that nothing was making any sense and then she left. Present-me can't reach her. Present-me has no clue what to do. I grab my cell from my desk. I check my messages. Again. "Your father will be home late." That's my dad's assistant. "Happy Fourth of July." Mom even included a smiley face. But she hasn't called.

My fingers hover over the screen. Maybe I could text Em.

Again.

It's been four days.

Four days and she hasn't been to the studio, she hasn't returned my calls, she hasn't updated any of her social media, she hasn't told Rob because when I saw him, he seemed totally oblivious. And I couldn't press without sounding suspicious. I flop on the bed, staring at the ceiling. Today, she won't be able to ignore me. It's the Fourth of July and Rob invited me to join them in Central Park.

I close my eyes. I've been up all night, checking online for more clues, checking Dad's office for any files that would help Em, checking her old pictures on Facebook. There's a bunch of the two of us:

dancing of course, but also jumping in the pool at their house in the Hamptons, laughing by the fire last year, on my birthday. I look happy in those pictures; she does too. And I'm starting to see why Jen always bitched about the time I was spending with Em, why all my girlfriends complain about her.

My cell rings, and I quickly sit up. Rob's calling—it's like he knows I'm having very inappropriate thoughts about his sister.

"Hey Nico," Rob says. "Can you do me a big favor?"

"I would say sure but the last time you asked me for a big favor, I almost got arrested."

He laughs. "Don't worry, it's not about helping me break into a lab." He pauses. "Can you stay with Em today?"

"I thought we were all going to chill in Central Park and wait for the fireworks. It's our first Fourth of July in the city."

"I wanted to. But Giovanni wants us to drive to Cape Cod for a few days. Come on, you met Giovanni. He's I-ta-lian." He emphasizes the last words as if that's supposed to explain everything. "Like not Little Italy, but Italy, my country."

I chuckle. "You were born here, your dad was born here, your grandfather was born here. You're more American than me, dude.'

"Whatever. I'm Italian and he's Italian and he's so hot and he's funny. And he's got this accent."

"Okay, I get it. No Fourth of July fireworks for you."

"Oh there might be. I'm hoping there will be." He laughs. "Anyways, Dad and Mom are trying to figure out some more financial stuff and it's tense in here. Em has been even more OCD than usual. And all of her friends are in the Hamptons." He sighs. "Nonna even has plans with someone she met at the market." He pauses and then repeats each word slower. "She's seventy and she has plans."

"I get it. You want to make sure your sister isn't alone." I pace around in my room.

"You're my last resort. Trust me."

"Thanks, I appreciate the vote of confidence." I pick up a collage Em made for my birthday last year—pictures of all of us, funny quotes and some of my official dancing photographs. That was the first time someone ever made something for me.

Rob whistles. "You know what I mean. She's been asking weird questions about her birth parents. Being even more evasive than usual. Dad's been mostly brushing her off and Mom goes into one of her sad moods whenever the topic comes up. Like it's her fault she couldn't have another baby."

"Does Em know you're bailing on her?"

"Not exactly. If she did, she'd cancel and she'd go dance or wallow in her room. You know how she is."

I even know how amazing her lips taste. I place the collage back on my bookshelf, tighten my grip on the phone and shake my head. I so don't need to think about this right now.

"Fine, I'll meet her by the little street vendor by the water."

"Great. You're the best."

"Tell me about it. Now, go have fun. And don't forget to practice your Italian."

"I'm about to perfect my Italian, trust me."

THE PARK IS FULL OF happy laughter and chatter. Em's smiling as she kicks a balloon back to a group of little kids playing soccer, but she freezes as soon as her eyes land on me. "Where's Roberto?" she asks from a distance. One guy is ogling her, but his girlfriend turns his head back to hers. I can't blame him. Her skirt may be long but with the slight breeze, it hikes up her legs at every step, showing only a little but giving so much to the imagination. And man, I'm turning creative. Her tank top is tight and light blue and definitely gives a good view of her small cleavage. Her boobs aren't huge but they're perfect. Her hair is flowing on her shoulders, and on her wrist she wears a leather bracelet. The leather bracelet I gave her for her birthday two years ago. The leather bracelet it took me weeks to find, because I wanted it to be perfect. Perfect for her.

She finally moves closer, but it's like each step is hard to take. She taps my shoulder with her finger before dropping her bag to her feet. "Hello? I tried to call him but he wouldn't pick up. I assumed we would all meet here."

I'm tempted to take her hand in mine and whisk her away.

But instead, I shrug. "There's an Italian guy."

"I should have known. He was talking about Giovanni and how he wanted to spend more time with him." She pauses as if she talked too much, as if we didn't know almost everything about one another, and my chest hurts. "I should go."

I gently touch her hand and when she doesn't move, I let my fingers trail on her arm. "Come on, Em. Let's relax. I've got a few drinks for us. Your favorite."

"Grape juice?"

I laugh, remembering how Em always had grape juice in her lunch boxes when we were kids and how she used to share it with me because Mom asked our maid to put veggie juices in mine. "Better than that."

She glances around and lowers her voice. "You didn't. How did you manage to get rum and Coke?"

I lean toward her too, whispering. "My parents' liquor cabinet is very well stocked."

She jolts back and crosses her arms on her chest—putting more distance between us again. "What are your parents doing today?" Her tone is a mix of worry and suspicion. I wish I could erase the frown on her face. It's like we're tiptoeing around the real topic that's scaring her and I'm fucking afraid that if I say the wrong word, she'll bolt away.

Instead, I keep the conversation casual. "Dad's having a party. And Mom's still enjoying her spa-cation."

"Hmmm," Em replies. She stares at her flip-flops and then chews one of her nails.

"Come on, there are still pretty good spots." I point to the grass almost already full. The weather is so humid, Em's hair has turned all frizzy, and I'm tempted to run one finger through it to see how the curls would feel. Em grabs her sunglasses from her oversized bag.

"I brought some sandwiches and some fruit." Her voice is tentative, but at least she's not running in the opposite direction.

I smile. "Then, we're good to go."

We settle on the grass, talking but not really talking, laughing but not really laughing, and we wait. We wait for the weirdness to dissipate. We wait for the fireworks, close to families and large group of peoples and lovers cuddling next to one another. Our hands touch a thousand times, they touch for short periods of time and then for longer ones, as if we're playing with fire, not sure if we want to burn.

CHAPTER 13 - EM

The world spins. And there are happy bubbles everywhere. "It's a blue one," I giggle, pointing to the sky.

Nick laughs. He's got a pretty laugh. A sexy laugh. A laugh I want to hear all the time. Or his voice—his voice is much deeper now than it used to be. And it's a hot voice. A voice that gives me tingles everywhere. "So blue," I say again.

I lean into him. He's warm.

"It's red," he says and kisses the top of my head.

I kick off my shoes and my fingers play drums on his thigh. "It's pretty," I tell him and then tilt my head so I can look at him. "Do you think my real mom's pretty like Amanda? Do you think it's that Claire Carter lady?" The words tumble out of my mouth and they're kind of slurred together. Or maybe they should be slurred together. That's an important question. I shake my head, concentrating on the way his green eyes are almost blue right now. "I didn't want to talk to you." I close my eyes. "I didn't want to see you. Why does your dad have information I don't? What does he know? Why..." I open my eyes again and then shake my head. "I don't want to think about it."

Nick says something but I can't hear him. I love the way my body feels against his, I love the way he smells—the faint cologne he's had since he turned sixteen. I love him. My chest expands and then constricts. I can't say that to him. No, no, no.

"Em," he whispers and his eyes cloud with worry.

I look up in the sky. "I like you," I whisper. "I really *really* like you." He tenses behind me and I know he's looking for an easy way out. I should feel hurt, or confused, or sad, or disappointed, or angry. But instead, I look at him, daring him to say something.

"We should get going," he says. And random laughter bursts out of me. I was trying to stay serious, I swear. And maybe my laugh sounds wrong, kind of like a sad clown's laugh.

"You don't like to talk about your feelings. You love to show up with one random girl after the other, but did you ever confide in them? Do they know you?" I slap my hand on my mouth. No-Filter-Em: that should be my nickname or my superhero name. No-Filter-Em to the rescue! I giggle at my own joke and sip a bit of my drink, but he gently takes it away. "I talk too much, don't I? It's like I don't have a filter. I mean, it's not that I don't have a filter. I don't want to have one with you. With you, I feel like I can talk about anything and you won't judge me, you won't make fun of me. Well, you might make fun of me. But not in a mean way." My stomach churns and I roll on my side, stretching, trying to make the feeling go away, but it's there and soon I feel like retching. "I think I'm going to get sick."

"Let's get you out of here." Nick jumps to his feet. Nick doesn't need a nickname, he acts like a superhero in my mind most of the times, except with all those girls. I hold on to my stomach. "Take my hand," he says and pulls me up. "The bathroom's over there."

"I won't make it." I moan and wobble to the side. There are only a few people scattered around. And I throw up in the bushes. "Oh my God, everything's spinning."

"You can do this, come on." He wraps an arm around my waist.

"I'm so sorry," I whimper. "I d-d-didn't mean to throw up like this." My steps are hesitant, and my stomach gurgles.

Nick stops suddenly and I'm about to protest that everything spins again, when he gently wipes my mouth with cold water. We're by one of the water fountains that joggers use, and he's wetting one of the napkins from my picnic basket into the splashing water. "You're fine. You'll be fine," he says so tenderly that I want to kiss him. But instead, I mutter, "I really do like you."

He smiles and leads me back to the streets. People pass by us, cars rush by. He drops the basket on the ground and still holding me, he picks up his cell with his other hand. "Hey John, can you come and pick me up? I'm on West Seventy-Seventh Street, by Central Park."

He hangs up quickly and then calls for one of the vendors close by. "I need a water bottle."

"I'm tired," I say and wiggle out of his embrace. "I need to sit." And I do. And I yawn. And I want to sleep so badly.

"Come on, drink some water," Nick says, crouching next to me. People are walking around us. I should get up. But my legs are so tired. I take a sip.

I hold on to his arm, drinking one more gulp.

"I don't know my limits. And that cocktail was good. So. Yums. I never say 'yums.' I usually say 'yummy.' It was yummy yums." This is funny. Yummy yums. I giggle but then sigh. "My stomach's still not happy."

Nick slowly caresses my forehead. And maybe I've closed my eyes for a second. "The car's here," he says. I'm still wobbly when I stand up.

The black sedan pulls in front of us.

And his father opens the door.

CHAPTER 14 – NICK

"What were you thinking? She's drunk! And if Dino sees her like this, he's going to lose it." Dad's clenching his fists and staring at me. He's usually calm-angry, not all full-out angry.

"She's tired," I lie, but I know we've taken it too far. The last two drinks were definitely too much for her. I tried to tell her, but she shushed me, and she was having so much fun.

"You are walking a thin line, Nicholas Everett Grawski. A very thin line."

"What is that supposed to mean? And I'm not twelve any-more—using my full name is not as intimidating." That's not entirely true. My dad still scares the crap out of me. Em's snoring on my shoulder and I don't want to wake her up, so I lower my voice. "What have you done, Father?"

His eyes widen for only a second before going back to his I'm-pissed-at-you frown. "What do you mean?"

"I heard you and Mom talk. About Em's adoption."

"You will keep your mouth shut. This is none of your business."

She stirs in her sleep and lets out one big snore. I can't help but smile a little.

"It is. Em is *my* business."

"Let it be, that's all I'm saying." He's using his I-can-get-you-in so much trouble tone, but for once in my life defying my father is not about testing boundaries, or about gaining something for my-

self, or about pushing his buttons. Defying him seems to be the only way to help her, and I'll do anything.

CHAPTER 15 – EM

"I told you to stay out of this!"

Distant voices stir me out of my restless sleep. My head pounds and I groan. It's like someone is doing jumps in it, and they're not even good jumps.

"And I told you I wanted answers. Em deserves answers." A door slams.

People shouldn't be arguing this early in the morning. Isn't there a rule about that somewhere?

What are Nick and his dad even doing in my house? I turn to my side with my eyes closed. Nick's dad never comes to my house anymore. He used to. He used to play golf with my dad, they used to talk about real estate investment and country clubs and all that jazz. But he never comes anymore. Never. Ever.

Before, I was certain it was because he felt guilty about my father losing his job. Now, I wonder if it doesn't have something to do with my adoption. I've never known he was involved in it, and my parents assured me they were "open" about the details.

This is not my bed. This bed is much larger. This bed has way too many pillows. This bed has silky sheets.

My eyes pop open. Definitely not my room.

"Shit!" I wince. I got totally wasted last night, and with Nick. Did I tell him I like him a lot? Did I kiss him? Again?

I struggle to remember his answer, but I'm pretty sure he didn't declare his undying love for me.

Note to self: Never get drunk with Nick. Again.

My parents are going to freak I didn't get home.

And his father came to pick us up. That's great. I struggle out of bed. I'm still in my dress from last night, and I cross my fingers this guest bedroom is on the first floor so I can escape without anyone noticing me.

Someone slams a door. Heavy steps get closer to my room.

A knock. "Em, are you up? I should bring you back home, or Rob is somehow going to find out you didn't come home, and he's going to drive back from Cape Cod and kill me."

Of course, let's worry about what my brother thinks. I want to be mad at Nick, I was mad at him after he told me what he overheard, but I have a fuzzy memory of him, wiping my mouth tenderly. Shit. Wiping my mouth from throw-up. That's one sexy scene he's not going to forget soon.

"Em?" he calls again.

"I'm up. I'm up."

The door cracks open and Nick steps inside, with breakfast on a tray. "You look like shit," he says and my stomach grumbles.

Nick sets the tray on the bed. He's got big shadows under his eyes and he's frowning.

I cringe. "Thanks. You don't look that great yourself today."

He turns to me, raises an eyebrow and laughs. A full-out belly laugh. I can't help but smile back. Seeing him somewhat happy is so much better.

"I got you some of the things I know you like: waffles and eggs. I've read somewhere that eggs are supposed to help a hangover."

"Thank you," I reply, my heart warming at his thoughtful gesture.

He nods and points to the door. "If you open that door on the left, you'll find a bathroom. You can take a shower or at least brush your teeth..."

I wince. "Is it that bad?"

"I can smell your breath from here, and it ain't pretty." He pulls a chair over and sits close to me.

"I'm sorry I drank so much."

"Don't worry... Those cocktails were pretty strong. And you're kind of a lightweight."

"Whatever. Don't tell Roberto I drank, okay/"

His eyes bore into mine and my heart skips a beat. I can't be imagining the electricity between us. I can't be imagining that he's looking at me like he wants to kiss me again, that he's been thinking about it ever since that day in the studio.

Okay, maybe he doesn't want to kiss me right at this moment, not now that I have the yuckiest breath on Earth, but something shifted yesterday. Maybe while we laughed, while we talked, or while we watched the fireworks in each other's arms. At least I think we did.

"Are you sure you're fine?" he asks.

"You can't answer my question with a question. That's illegal. That should be one of our rules. Always answer questions honestly."

"Fine. I won't tell Roberto you drank...unless he asks."

I nod and wince again. "And I'm not fine. My head is about to split in half." I pause. "Did your dad tell you anything? I heard you fighting with him."

"He didn't tell me shit. He keeps on telling me to mind my business."

"Maybe if I'm the one to ask him?" I whisper. "Maybe he would tell me what he knows?"

"You can try, but I don't think that's going to work." He's hiding something. His face's a bit closed off, but then it opens again. "Maybe you could ask your dad about it."

"I need to grow some lady balls. It's funny how when I started to look, I had this fairy tale in my mind and now I'm scared to go forward, I'm scared of the answers," I admit. "That's why I didn't talk to you last week. I knew if I saw you, we would end up talking about it. That, and I was weirded out about the fact your dad was involved in all this."

"Tell me about it." He rubs the back of his neck and I glance at the tray, nibble on a waffle. He did that for me. He's fighting with his dad for me. He's there for me.

My heart beats faster, remembering yesterday. What did he answer when I told him I liked him?

I could ask him. I could simply go ahead and ask him if maybe, maybe he likes me too. If we were still in sixth grade I could pass him a note.

Why can't I ask him? I kissed him the other day and it was a pretty amazing kiss. He kissed me back. I know he did. If I hadn't played it off, we might still be making out now. Days later, we would have never left the dance studio. Maybe, he never would have told me about what he overheard. Maybe it would have all been simpler.

"There, I brought you an aspirin too. It should help." Instead of dropping it in my open palm, he carefully sets it on the tray, as if he's afraid we could inadvertently touch.

"I'm going to take a quick shower and brush my teeth." I stand up. And then turn to him. Wanting to say something. Wanting to ask him. Wanting to hear his answer.

Nick clears his throat. "I'll wait for you downstairs."

He stands up, and hurries out of the room without another word.

Maybe it's an unspoken answer to my unspoken question.

CHAPTER 16 – NICK

"Let me walk you." I lean against the door as Em puts on her flip-flops. "Let me do the gentleman thing here." I smile my most charming smile, the one that usually gets me out of trouble easily.

"I need some time alone," she says.

"You're breaking my heart," I tease her, but I'm not getting the expected reaction.

"Am I?" she mutters, looking up at me and then glancing away. "I can walk the ten minutes by myself. I need a bit of time anyways." She pauses. "I'll call you after I talk to them."

"Okay. I'm going to talk to my dad again. Not that I have high hopes for what he's going to tell me." We stand in front of one another awkwardly.

I've never noticed until now how much preparation or thought there is behind saying goodbye to someone. Should I hug her? And if I hug her, for how long? And I think Em got my balls tied somewhere in her bag.

She leans forward at the same time as I do and we barely avoid a head-on collision. This time, she smiles and it's genuine and it's making it difficult to not pull her to me. Like this morning, in the guest bedroom. She's going through such a tough time and all I think about it tasting her lips again, feeling her body underneath mine, making her laugh, discovering every inch of her skin, forgetting the real world and creating our own.

She grabs her picnic basket and kisses my cheek quickly before hurrying out of the door. My eyes follow her silhouette until she disappears around the corner.

"Nick!" my father yells from his office. He's been here all along and he hasn't even come out to acknowledge Em's presence. Way to go, Dad. Way to show me how to be a man.

"Nicholas!" he calls again and I slam the door.

"What?"

"I need to talk to you." His voice sounds super calm, and it's always a bad omen when he's too Zen.

I'm tempted to ignore him. Ignoring him would only anger him though, so that might not be the best strategy.

"I'm coming," I reply and drag my feet past the dining room into his large office. His diplomas are all over the wall and above the fireplace, he has a portrait of his own father, the one who started Grawski & Sons. He's staring at me like I've done something wrong. Pretty much the same look my father has right now.

"We need to talk, son. Please, sit down," he says, gesturing to one of the two empty leather chairs in front of his imposing desk. I lick my dry lips. Em's kiss seems so far away. "What's going on?" I ask.

He taps his index finger on the globe standing by his lamp. He's the one who asked to see me, who summoned me in here, who made it seem like it was urgent, but now he has all the time in the world. One of his many tactics. He stops tapping and purses his lips before answering. "I understand you want to have fun this summer, but is Emilia really the best choice you have?"

"You used to like Emilia and her family," I reply.

"Used to being the operative words here, son. And I need you to think very carefully about all of this."

"Do you need be to be so careful because of Em's adoption? Why don't you answer me? Why don't you tell me why you even know something about it?"

"This has nothing to do with her adoption. And her adoption has nothing to do with what I'm telling you right now. Em's a good girl. She's smart and pretty, I get it. But she's not the one for you. She has a lot of baggage, and her future is uncertain." He pauses. "You and I have a deal."

I cringe but nod.

"Do I need to remind you that if you do not fulfill your side of the agreement, I will stop all donations to the school, I will stop paying your tuition, I will step down as member of the foundation."

"I remember," I reply. If he steps down as member of the foundation, I'm pretty sure my career will be doomed. It would be hard to hire someone whose father brought down such a prestigious institution like the School of Performing Arts. And I have no doubt he would do it without blinking.

"You're supposed to actually show up at work this summer. You're only interning three days a week—that's not a lot."

"I know. And I'm sorry. I'll be there on Monday."

"Fine." He crosses his arms. "I also wanted to talk to you about your mother."

"We should go see her. We used to go see her when she went to the spa. Make a field trip out of it."

He sets his elbows on the desk, leaning forward. "I don't have time. Work is very busy."

"Driving from New York to Connecticut takes about two to three hours. It's not that far and if we go with the driver, you could still work in the car." I hate my voice for sounding needy. Like I'm back to being a ten-year-old begging for him to go trick-or-treating with me.

He blinks once, but then leans back in his chair. "Your mother and I are having some issues."

"I know." I lean back in mine, mirroring his gesture. I know all his tactics to destabilize the person in front of him and I won't let him win.

He clears his throat—very unlike him. "We're thinking about getting separated for a bit."

"I know," I say again, staring at him, analyzing his face to see if there's any hint of regret. There's nothing. Only exasperation that I don't do as he pleases.

"Anyways. Enough about that." He pauses. "I have something else to ask you."

I don't like where this is going. He only asks me to do stupid things for his job: run errands, show up at fundraisers, and spend time with the daughters of possible clients. Like Jen five months ago. Like Maria ten months ago. I do change girlfriends very easily and he's not to blame, but some of those girls I only dated because of him.

"I need you to entertain Jen again."

Shit. I can't do that now. Not with everything that's going on with Em.

I raise an eyebrow. "Are you pimping me out?"

"Watch your mouth." He squares his shoulders and leans forward on his desk again, boring his eyes into mine and tapping his fingers on the lamp. "I'm only reminding you of our deal."

I don't want to think about our deal. Not when it can hurt Emilia,

"Our deal was for me to behave and to think about my options. Not to screw some random girl because you said so."

Dad slams his fist on the desk in a rare outburst of emotion. "I never asked you to screw her. I would never ask you to do anything like that. I only want you to remember that you have duties here too. It's not only do-as-you-please at your dance school, it's not only about what Nick wants!"

"That's right, it's all about what you want. Dino wasn't helping you with your shitty deals anymore so you fired him. I'm not doing as you please, so what, you're going to fire me too?"

"Don't tempt me, Nick. Do. Not. Tempt. Me." His tone is back to being super calm, very even.

"Whatever."

"And let me tell you something else. You stay out of Dino's affairs. You're so narrow-minded. You think you have all the answers? You have none. You leave Claire out of everything and you leave Emilia alone."

I bow to him as graciously as possible. "Yes, sir. Yes."

And then turn on my heels and slam the door.

CHAPTER 17 - EM

"Hi honey," Mom says when I enter the kitchen. I haven't even changed yet, and she frowns. "Hope you had fun yesterday. Luckily, Nick texted me to let me know you were staying over there."

Oh, that's why I didn't have thousands of voice mails or frantic messages. "It was...interesting," I reply and Dad raises an eyebrow.

"Roberto told us you and Nick ended up going to the fireworks by yourself. But he didn't say anything about you spending the night. We didn't know until almost midnight that you were going to sleep in his guest bedroom." Dad emphasizes the word "guest." "It was okay for you two to do that when you were ten, but you're older now. I don't think it's such a good idea to spend the night at Nick's." Dad can't even look me in the eyes.

Mom clears her throat. "What your father is trying to say...is..."

"Did you ever have that conversation with Roberto?" My voice sounds pissy, but I can't help but fume. I didn't have a good night's sleep. I can't remember half of yesterday and no one wants to answer my questions. Dad must know more than what he lets on. And now this BS?

"Emilia," Dad replies.

"I mean it. Roberto used to not come home for an entire weekend. And I only recall you telling him to be careful. And to have fun. Those were your words. Why can't I be careful and have fun too? Whatever it is you meant?" My voice rises. "And let's not tiptoe around every single topic. You don't want me to hang out with Nick."

"Em!" Mom protests. She shakes her hand. "We do want you to be careful. To be careful with your feelings. Nicholas is great, but..."

"Nick is the only one who's speaking the truth to me. He's the only who's trying to help me find my real parents." I look down, not wanting to see the way my mom flinches, not wanting to see the way my father's eyes widen, not wanting to see how my words hurt.

"We told you we would help you. We *are* helping you," Mom says, her voice faltering and my heart breaking.

"Em, do not use this tone with us." Dad stands up. I've forgotten how tall and imposing he is, but I won't back down. Not this time.

"Do you remember Claire Carter, Dad? And why does Nick's father have documents about my adoption?"

Dad's mouth gapes open for only a second, but I see it. I see he's taken aback. Mom shakes her head. "What are you talking about? Nick's dad helped us with some of the paperwork for your adoption. But that's the legal part of it—he doesn't know anything else." She chews on her lip. "And Claire was your father's assistant a long time ago; what does she have to do with anything?"

I cross my arms on my chest. "Yes, Dad. What does Claire Carter have to do with anything?"

"I don't know what you and Nick think you have uncovered but you're ridiculous, both of you!" He sounds annoyed but then he takes a deep breath as if to calm himself. He sits back down, and attempts to smile soothingly at my mom. "Nick's dad helped with some of the paperwork. And Claire was my assistant at the time."

"That's bullshit!" I say and wince. I never curse in front of my parents. "There's more to it than this and you know it. Mom doesn't but you know it. And I'm going to find out what it is."

I hurry out of the room, stomp up the stairs to the sound of my father telling me I'm grounded, of Mom asking him what's going on, and I slam the door.

I START UP MY COMPUTER and type "Claire Carter" and "Wraswki & Son." Her LinkedIn profile shows up. I click on it. She's pretty: she's got brown hair, kind of like mine. I lean closer. Could she be my mother? And what would it mean? Oh my God, did Dad have an affair with her? Is that it? Is that why Mom's not supposed to know?

I shiver and close the laptop. Maybe I shouldn't dig any deeper. Maybe I'm about to fuck up everything more than it already is. Maybe, I'm going to hurt the people I love.

I lie down on my comforter, thinking about all possibilities. Again. Maybe she's only the one who took care of the paperwork. My cell rings and I smile, seeing Rob's face on the display. I need a distraction and I need brotherly advice. "I'm so happy you're calling. How is Cape Cod?"

He sighs loudly. "Drop the act, Em. One, why on Earth did you sleep at Nick's last night?"

"Because I got drunk." I can't help but sound defensive.

"This is getting better and better."

"And you sound like Dad."

"Well, maybe he has a point."

I stand up and pace around the room. "That's funny because you didn't seem to think he had a point when he first forbade you to date Jim."

"That was different and you know it. Jim was dealing drugs."

I roll my eyes. "And Nick is what?"

"Nick can't keep a girlfriend longer than a few weeks. Nick's dad fired ours."

I want to scream. "You still talk to Nick. That has nothing to do with that."

"It doesn't, but that means you should understand Dad a bit more. He's afraid for you. We're worried for you. We know what's best for you."

I hang up. I can't hear this any longer. Everyone's lying and pretending.

Everyone tells me what I should do. I change into comfier clothes, grab my gym bag and head back downstairs. Mom and Dad are no longer in the kitchen and I know Mom's going to come and check on me very soon.

Even if I'm pissed, I still don't want them to worry. I grab the notepad by the phone and scribble, "Gone to the School."

And I head out, texting Nick. "I'm on my way to rehearse. Come?"

I'm going to be the one deciding what's best for me.

CHAPTER 18 - NICK

My father wanted me to come to some sort of meeting with him, some teleconference he's having with partners from London. He doesn't know what a day off is, and if he thinks we can forget our conversation and move on, he's delusional.

I push open the door of the rehearsing room. Em's already there, listening to her iPod playlist on the stereo—the one I made for her when we were hanging out during winter break. She's dancing as if all movements mean the world to her, as if if she stops dancing she's going to fall apart.

"That was amazing!" I tell her when the music stops.

"Whatever. It's all bullshit." She's sweating and breathing hard.

"What's wrong?"

"Nothing. Everything is great, wonderful, splendid."

But her voice is breaking.

I step closer to her, closer until I'm so close that I can touch her. One of my hands falls on her shoulder. She doesn't stiffen like I thought she would. I tilt her head toward me with my other hand.

"What's wrong?" I ask for the second time.

"Nothing," she whispers and I'm about to call her on her bullshit, when her gaze focuses on my lips. The last time that happened we had the best make-out session of my life.

She wraps one hand behind my neck and whispers, "I remember yesterday, I told you I really, really like you."

"Hmm. I remember," I reply and then even though I know I shouldn't be kissing her, there's no way in hell I'm pushing her away. She's too close, too intoxicating, too fucking sexy. When her lips brush mine, it's like we're both on fire. It's like our lips have been waiting to meet again, waiting to be together again, never wanting to let go.

I'm hard instantly. And when she whispers my name, I get lost in the moment. I nudge her mouth open and kiss her like I always wanted to, with everything I've kept bottled up for the past year, like it could be our last kiss. It should be our last kiss, but I can't get enough. My hands roam her back and then she's against the mirror, and one of her leg wraps around my waist.

And I'm about to explode. She molds to my body so perfectly and I love the way she feels in my arms, like she belongs there.

But then, I remember my rules. I remember I'm not supposed to be kissing her. I remember my promises to Roberto. I remember she feels insecure and sad right now. I pull back gently.

She bites her lip—that's what she does when she's unsure. I kiss her one last time, a small peck, something to reassure her that I don't regret kissing her. Because I don't. But I'm not sure what to do.

She runs her hand down my back, slowly. Teasing and tender. But her voice sounds so tired when she says, "If you tell me you can't kiss me because of my brother I'm going to kill you. I had a shitty day. And I can't take one more rejection."

"Kissing you seems like the only thing that makes sense to me right now."

"Oh." She smiles.

"But you know I can't have a relationship. I can't. Once school starts again, I'm going to have to work even harder than now. And my parents, it's complicated. And yes, your brother clearly would kill us, he would kill me if he found out."

"How about we forget all of that, all of this for the summer? One summer and then we go back to being friends, and that's it. Nothing more, nothing less."

"You deserve so much more than that," I reply even though I can picture it, even though she deserves much more. She fucking deserves the world.

But, one summer together. One summer in the city while everyone we know is away. One summer to help her deal with whatever she finds.

One summer.

CHAPTER 19 - EM

Nick stays silent for a second too long. And I step aside, away from his arms. I can't deal with someone else telling me what's good for me, what I should do, what I need, what I want. I know what I want.

He gently tugs me back to him, until our bodies press against one another again.

"You deserve everything," Nick says.

I tilt my head to look into his eyes. "I know what I want. And I want you. You're the only one who doesn't bullshit me." I pause. "You could say no, you could tell me that you want a real relationship, but it's not true. You could say no, because you think you might hurt me, but let me make that decision. Don't make it for me. Because, I'm already hurting." My anger fades away and there's only raw pain in my voice. "You're the only one who helps me, who's standing by my side even when I screw up." I pause and take a deep breath. "And you're right, we can't date. Not really. I mean, we can't be together while we're at school."

He raises an eyebrow like I'm full of shit, but he's right. My fairy-tale romance is too good to be true, and I'll get what I can—but under my own rules. I continue. "It's going to be too complicated, too many expectations, and then what happens if we don't work? Then what? We pass each other in the hallways, I see you with your flavor of the hour, with your *arabesque* of the minute, and

I say nothing? At least, with an expiration date, we both know what we're getting into."

"My *arabesque* of the minute?" he kisses my neck and my body tingles. "I'm not that bad."

"Who are you kidding? You've dated half of Manhattan."

His shoulders slump. "I haven't. I don't think I have."

"You never lie. You never make false promises. The majority of girls think they can change you. The majority of girls believe that they're the one you're going to change your ways for." And as the words cross my well-kissed lips, my heart tightens into a knot that's every sailor's dream. Is this what I want? Is it what I hope will happen? I shake my head. I only want to feel his lips on mine again, his body pressing against mine.

"Are you sure you want to do this?" he asks again. His fingers caress my cheek slowly, like he wants to memorize it in case I disappear in a pirouette.

"I am," I reply, thinking I'm strong enough to handle this. I'm strong enough to end this when needed. I'm not going to cling to him. I'm not going to ask him to stay with me when the summer draws to a close. Even if it breaks my heart.

CHAPTER 20 - NICK

When Em invited me to her Nonna's restaurant on Monday, I sweated my balls off. I'm so not ready for the big family dinner, I can't face Roberto or Em's parents. But Em explained her Nonna is going on another date with the older gentleman she met at the market. Em says her Nonna believes in love, she believes her deceased husband sent that guy to her to make her dance again. So, they're going to one of those festivals the firefighters organize every summer. The way Em blushed when she talked about love made me want to tease her, made me want to make her smile.

But I resisted. I can't cross the line—what we have is a friendship with temporary and limited benefits. Nothing less. Nothing more. And I better remind myself of that before I do or say something stupid. I'm tempted to throw away the flowers I got from a street merchant on the way to Brooklyn. It's a bouquet of tulips, and there's something about them that reminds me of Em.

And oh my God, where did my balls go? I've never been so touched by anyone, so in synch with anyone in my entire life.

Before I can convince myself to turn around and cancel our date tonight, I ring the bell of the restaurant, hiding the flowers behind me.

"You can come in!" Em calls, her voice a tad muffled. "In the kitchen!" she says again and I follow her voice.

She's covered in flour, almost from head to toe. Her dark brown curly hair is peppered with white. And she's holding a cannoli in her hand.

"What are you doing?" I chuckle, still holding the flowers behind me.

She steps closer to me. "You're not going to be laughing once I get flour all over you too."

She kisses me gently but too quickly for my taste. "Screw the flour," I tell her and bring her closer to me with one of my hands for a real kiss, a deep I-want-more kiss. She moans in my mouth and I'm suddenly forgetting why it's a bad idea to take it further than our make-out sessions, why I can't cross that line with her if I can't promise her more than this summer.

But luckily, she steps away from me, before my lower brain decides to overcome my real one.

"What are you hiding?" She's smiling that bright smile of hers, the one that touches both brains of mine.

I run my hand through my short hair and then shift on my feet. I've never been this nervous with a girl before. I hand her the flowers. "Hmm. A guy was pushing those outside the subway. For you." I don't tell her that I thought of her as soon as I saw them or that I was worried she might not like tulips.

She takes them carefully and gazes at them with the tenderness she sometimes has when she looks at me.

Shit. I am in trouble.

"I love them. Thank you." She kisses my cheek and then skips to the other side of the messy kitchen to get a small vase. She arranges the flowers in it and then turns back to me.

"I made lasagna this afternoon. For us. And then I've been try-ing to make my Nonna's cannoli for dessert, but I've been having issues."

She blows a strand of hair away from her face, or at least she tries to, but it keeps on falling back. "What type of issues?" I ask.

"It doesn't taste the same," she replies and pulls out a tray full of delicious-looking creamy pastries. "Here, taste one." I plop it in my mouth and it's my turn to moan. Those pastries are absolutely amazing.

"Those are wonderful." I stare at her lips. "Like you." I want to forget about the pastries, and the dinner, and everything else right now. I want to carry her onto the nearby counter and see where it takes us. But then she switches topic and it calms me down as quickly as a cold shower.

"Roberto's pissed at me."

"For what?" I tilt my head and tighten my fists.

"Don't sound so scared, it's not about you." I cock an eyebrow. Rob called me on July 5th to tell me to stay away from Em if I couldn't offer her forever. We talked about it and I somewhat came to a truce with him. She bites her lip. "Fine, it's still a bit about you. But mainly, it's about me not giving up on looking for my birth par-ents. Despite what Dad said about Claire Carter." She pauses and picks up another pastry before dropping it into her mouth. If she licks those lips one more time, I will forget my promises to myself. "Maybe he's right though. Like what else do I know? Based on her LinkedIn profile, she's an executive assistant for Procter & Gam-ble now. But all I have is what you overheard, and I'm so fucking scared."

"What do you mean?"

"Didn't you ever get so close to something you really wanted only to have taken it away from you?"

You. But that's my own fault, so instead I reply, "Yes. Remember the lead at last year's showcase? It was mine for only five minutes."

"That's because you were only a junior then—they don't give leads to juniors."

"I'm sure you or Nata could get the lead."

She frowns. "Is the flour getting to your brain? Maybe Nata, but not me."

"Whatever. You know you're good and with us practicing every day, you're getting even better!" I pause. "I couldn't find anything in my dad's office yet, and this week might be tough because he's working from home a lot, but next week, we could try to dig deeper in there. There's some important conference. He wanted me to come with him, as part of my stupid internship, but I told him no."

"You never talk about it. About your work there."

Because I don't want to tell you about Jen. Because I don't want to show you how low I can go to get what I want. Because I'm afraid you're not going to look at me with so much passion in your eyes.

I purse my lips. "Not much to say. Dad put me in an office with a real intern, one who graduated from Harvard Law and who wanted to get into business. All I do all day is listen to him talk about how awesome my father is, and how he wants to become like him. Luckily it's only three days a week and I get to leave early."

"Sounds like fun." She nudges me and I capture her hand in mine, bring it to my lips and gently kiss it.

"No, this is fun." I kiss her cheek, then her lips. "This is amazing." I kiss her neck. "This is fucking amazing." I steal one of her pastries. "I promise you, Em. I'll help you in any way I can. And I'll make sure you smile at least once a day."

She giggles, blushing. "Why is that?"

"Because seeing you smile is making everything better. Everything."

This time, when I kiss her, I don't hold anything back. We may only have one summer, but it's going to be a summer like no other.

CHAPTER 21 - EM

A few days later, I still can't believe Nick and I are somewhat of an item. I still can't believe that I'm so much closer to finding my birth mom. I still can't believe how everything can change in the blink of an eye.

"Where are you going?" Roberto asks me as I'm about to head out.

"If I tell you the truth, are you going to lecture me or are you going to tell me to have fun and to say hi to Nick?" I cock my head to the side, watching his reaction.

He sighs but pulls me to him for a quick hug. "Have fun, say hi to Nick." He pauses. "He knows I'll kill him if he hurts you."

I roll my eyes, but my chest feels much lighter, knowing I don't have to hide from Roberto. I give him a quick kiss on the cheek. "I'm happy. And that's what counts, right?" I pause. "Plus, you said yourself that you were enjoying every second with Giovanni because he has to go back to Italy at the end of the summer. I'm sure you understand."

His smile is sad. "Yes, but both Giovanni and I would love to make it work. We're not going into it with an expiration date on our relationship."

I flinch, but then shake my head. "I'm not saying I won't cry at the end of the summer, but let me be. Let me make my own mistakes, especially when they don't feel like mistakes. At all."

He hugs me again, but this time, it's warmer, more protective. "Be careful, that's all I'm asking."

"You too," I tell him and skip out of the house, before Mom has a chance to join in the discussion. I haven't talked much with my parents ever since that day I threw Claire Carter in their faces. I'm still hoping they'll come around.

I know they'll come around.

But for now, my heart hammers in my chest as I hurry to the School of Performing Arts, where I have a date with Nick.

FOR ONCE, NICK'S ARRIVED before me and for once, I get to watch him as he leaps in the air, as his muscular torso bends to the side, as he moves in such a way that my entire body flames up. He's not only hot, he's super sexy. He's mesmerizing. He's looking at me.

I clear my throat. "Nice moves," and I think my face gets even redder.

His laugh is happy and warm and does things to me I can't explain. The way he looks at me like I'm everything to him, the way he strides my way, still not wearing a shirt.

He leans in and his mouth meets mine for a kiss that's both sweet and explosive, a kiss that leaves me breathless.

His arms wrap around my waist and he pulls me off the ground like it's nothing. "Are you ready to spin?" He chuckles. He used to make me spin when we were younger, make me fly in the air until I begged him to stop. But not this time. I press my lips to his again. "I'm ready whenever you are."

And I laugh as he turns and turns and turns, until we're both begging for mercy. He gently drops me back on the floor and leans against the wall. "Let's dance but let's not rehearse," he says.

"What do you want to dance?"

"I just want to feel you," he replies and takes my hand in his. The music playing is a piece by Mozart. It's fast but Nick's going slow; he settles his body against mine and he starts waltzing. I smile, because I remember him saying one time to whatever girl he was with that he loves dancing, but that she'd never get him to waltz for no reason.

And with the way he's smiling, I know he remembers too. I know he's giving me something special without saying it. And I close my eyes, let myself fall into the music and into the movement.

With him.

CHAPTER 22 – NICK

Every morning, I ask Daddy Dearest for more information about Em's adoption. Every morning, he shuts me down. Every morning, he reminds me of my duties as his son, as his heir. But this morning is different. Mom's birthday is today.

"Are we going to see her this weekend?" I ask before popping a piece of toast in my mouth.

"I'm busy this weekend," he replies, not looking away from The Wall Street Journal. "Did you hear about what's going on in the euro area right now? Some analysts fear a contagion of the crisis to other markets. Between that and the talks of stricter financial regulations everywhere, our investments could take a hit. That and we might need to change the way we conduct our business."

"It sounds fascinating." I don't even think he realizes I'm being ironic. He takes one more sip of his coffee and stands up.

"Don't forget you have to work tomorrow," he says.

"I know. I won't forget," I reply and then add, "Why don't you show us the paperwork from Em's adoption? She does have a birth certificate, so you must have the rest of the paperwork."

"I told you. This is none of your business and I'm bound by client privileges, as you will be too once you realize your career as a dancer is not what you want for your life."

"You mean what you want for my life." I take another bite, so used to this conversation it doesn't even faze me anymore. "Have a good day. I'll see you later."

He pauses for a second, looking at me, and I hate that we have the same eyes. I hate that I get my height from him. I hate that I still want him to accept me for who I am, to help me, to help Mom. "See you soon, son."

And like that he's out of the house and out of my life. As always.

EM ARRIVES ALMOST AS soon as I call her. She's wearing one of those sundresses that is meant to be taken off slowly. But we're going to see Mom, so not really the direction my thoughts should take.

"Are you sure you want to come with me?"

"Of course! It's your mom's birthday, she's going to be so happy to see you!" She gives me a hug; it's spontaneous and it's not a friendly-hug, it's a full-body hug, and I think she's as surprised as me by it. But when she pulls away, I tug her back to me and melt into her embrace.

"Let's get going." I kiss her gently on the lips. Like we've been doing this for years instead of weeks.

On the road, we play stupid games, like finding random license plates from California and Alaska, or we look for signs where the city starts with B. We listen to music, sing out loud and then we play Twenty Questions.

During the trip, my hand casually falls on her thigh and my fingers trace circles underneath her dress. She tenses at first but then she pulls her dress a bit higher up. I have to restrain myself to simply take the next exit, and park somewhere.

But then, she takes my hand in hers, and intertwines our fingers. Her skin's so soft and she smells like peaches, and flowers and summer.

The GPS lets me know I need to turn right. "I didn't tell her we were coming."

"Why?" Em asks.

"Because I didn't want her to tell me I couldn't come. Because I didn't want her to lie to my face about what I overheard."

"It's her birthday, she hasn't seen you in a while. Don't ruin it for her," Em says and I squeeze her hand. "Your father seems to be the one who knows more about my adoption than she does. It's killing me to say that, but don't mention anything to your mom. Not today. Definitely not today." She pauses. "For me. Don't ask anything."

"I..." I clear my throat. "I know." That's not what I wanted to say. At all.

THE SPA WHERE MOM IS staying is even bigger than what I remember. More grandiose. We park by the entrance and a valet picks up my keys. "Nice car," he says of my classic Mustang.

"Thank you," I reply. It's a 1968 black Mustang coupé—it used to be my grandfather's. He bought it for next to nothing back in the day and he's the one who repaired it. My father gave it to me when I turned sixteen.

I open the door for Em and hold her hand as we walk up the stairs, to the receptionist who is sitting behind an imposing counter and a bunch of white flowers. "Hi, I'd like to see Mrs. Grawski."

Her lips turn up in a smile. "You must be her son. She talks about you all the time."

"I am."

"And this is your girlfriend, I presume?"

I don't know what to say. I don't know what to reply. I don't know what's wrong with me. One summer, man. One summer is all you get.

"Do you know where we can find Mrs. Grawski?" Em asks, saving me from answering the question.

"She's currently in painting class. You can walk through this hallway to the right," the receptionist says. "But let me call first."

I let go of Em's hand and she frowns, but then smiles again. "I can see why your mom loves to come here. It's so peaceful: the soft music, the high ceilings, the mountains all around."

"It is definitely more peaceful than the war zone at home."

The receptionist hangs up the phone and gestures to the beige couches. "Mrs. Grawski will step out of her painting class to welcome you."

Before we can even sit, I hear mom's voice. "Nicholas!" She hurries our way. Em tenses next to me but I whisper, "Thanks for being here. Thanks for coming."

I stand up and hug Mom. It's quick and formal but it's still a hug. "Happy Birthday, Mom!"

"Where is your father?" she asks and my shoulders slump. Why does it have to be the first thing she asks? Not a "how are you?" or anything. But then she gives me another hug. "He's probably working. I'm so happy you drove all the way. That's the best birthday gift." And she sounds happy. Really happy to see me. I relax.

"Em came with me," I say, and Em stands up.

"You're even lovelier than what I remember, Emilia." Mom air-kisses Em's cheeks and then glances at me "Are you two finally an item?"

I frown, but before I can answer Em blabbers, "We've been hanging out."

Oh. So that's the explanation we're giving people. Good to know. Fuck, why did I want to proudly announce, *Yes, we're finally dating and it's awesome.*

Mom puts her hand on my forearm. "Let's go drink some tea, outside. There is such a nice breeze up here."

She links her other arm with Em, and, together, we go drink tea. We go and pretend that there's nothing wrong with this picture and that everything is great.

We're good at pretending.

CHAPTER 23 – EM

The drive back from the spa was more silent, less festive and when Nick dropped me off at Nonna's, I kissed him with as much tenderness as I could. I wanted him to come eat dinner with us tonight, but he wants to go home. He's tired. And I think he's more worried about his parents' marriage than he's letting on.

I push Nonna's restaurant door open.

"Emilia! Bellissima, this dress is beautiful! You look so happy." Nonna hugs me and I relish in her embrace—it's so much warmer than the hug Nick got from his mom. Once more, I realize how lucky I am. She winks. "Does that smile have to do with the amount of time you're spending with Nicholas?"

"Nonna," I say and then kiss her cheek. "How is it going with Mr. Edwards?"

"A lady never kisses and tells," she replies, laughing, and I follow her in the kitchen.

"What's for dinner tonight?"

"Pasta Bolognese. Come on, everyone's already here."

And I step inside the restaurant. I wave to the regulars and stroll between customers to sit at our table.

"Hi," I say.

"Em, I want you to meet Giovanni," Roberto says, and a tall boy who has one of the warmest smiles I've ever seen stands up.

"Very nice to meet you," he says and his accent is as warm as his smile.

I sit down between Mom and Giovanni. Mom squeezes my hand. "I'm sorry we're hitting a rough patch. But I meant what I told you, darling. I will help you as much as I can. We're not lying to you."

Maybe *you*'re not, I think, but don't say anything.

Instead, I look at the people gathering around the table and smile. Because, right now, as confused as I am, I'm grateful they're my family.

THREE DAYS LATER, I meet Nick after his internship. The temperatures are still soaring, but when he gives me a quick hug, I don't want it to end.

We start strolling in no particular direction. "Let's go to Central Park," Nick suggests and his arm brushes against mine. Our eyes meet and we both smile. It's funny how we've danced and kissed and kissed and kissed, but a simple touch still makes me breathless.

We don't hold hands in public. Especially so close to where people might see us. And even though I've been trying to pretend I don't care, my chest constricts. I stare at my feet for a second.

"Everything okay?" he asks.

"Fine," I lie, thinking about what Roberto told me the other day, how he and Giovanni don't have an expiration date on their relationship, how they looked so happy and in love yesterday. Our relationship is doomed in a few short weeks.

Nick bumps his hip to mine. "Do you want an ice cream? Come on, Em, you love Grom's pistachio ice cream. We could go to their shop by Colombus Circle." His hand touches my back briefly and I want to lean into him, I want to feel his arm around me.

"Ice cream, it is." I shake my head from all unwanted thoughts.

If only our relationship was as easy as a lick of ice cream.

CHAPTER 24 – NICK

While we chill under a tree in Central Park, I get a text from Dad that he will be leaving for a meeting late afternoon, and he won't be home for dinner. Not like I usually expect him to be home for dinner. Not that we had dinner together in the past months. But whatever. That might be his way of trying to reconnect, but it's really the perfect opportunity to check his desk at his oversized home office more thoroughly.

We hurry back to my place.

We walk in front of his office, and the door's wide open. He's sorting through a bunch of papers. "Good afternoon, Emilia," he says and she startles.

"Good afternoon, sir." She never called my father by his first name. And I guess she's not about to start now. The way her hands are curled up into fists by her side and the way she's pursing her lips are clear signs that she's pissed, but trying to contain her anger.

My father clears his throat. "I understand you went with my son to visit my wife. She was happy to see you. She was happy to see him. Thank you for doing that."

Em turns to me for a second with eyes so wide I wonder if she's seeing things I can't. Then, she looks at my father, her eyes narrowing like she's trying to figure him out. "I think it was important for Nick."

My father tilts his head to the side. "Indeed you're right. And I should have been there."

Say what? What is going on?

Em nods and even though her shoulders have relaxed, her posture is still tense. She squeezes my hand. "Yes, you should have. Have a good day, sir."

"Emilia?" my dad calls again. "Your parents did a great job raising you. Never forget that."

"Thank you, and I never will."

"Don't stay up too late, kids. We don't want a repeat from the Fourth of July," Dad says and I think he's almost smiling.

We hurry up the stairs into my room, and I turn to Em. "That was hot. You telling my dad exactly how it is took some guts. And man you're sexy when you're angry."

She smiles and I put my arms around her, her back against the door. "I want to kiss you so badly right now."

"So, why don't you?" She licks her lips.

"Because if I kiss you right now, in my bedroom..."

"Pssh...don't overthink this," she says and pulls me to her. Our lips collide and our tongues dance together. Her hand trails down my back and sneaks underneath my shirt.

I slow the kiss down, enjoying the way she tastes, the way she touches me. My own hands caress her, and I want to feel her closer. I want to feel all of her. I force myself to stop kissing her for a second. "You're killing me," I say and she smiles again—this time her smile is more shy, less self-assured, and I kiss her again to show her how much I want this, how much I want her.

Both of my hands cup her face and I deepen the kiss until she moans.

And then, I tug her, walking backwards until my calves hit my bedframe. She falls on top of me and if I don't stop or think about something gross right now—my parents having sex, ewww—I will explode here and there. It's not my first time, far from it, but it almost feels like it.

She peppers kisses on my neck. She's breathing hard and her hand tentatively goes further down and down and down. And I'm going to combust.

I turn so that I'm now on top of her, holding my weight on my forearms. Her face is flushed, her mouth is half open.

"We can continue—please tell me you want to continue," I say and I watch her reaction, I don't want to push her. She's staring at me like she wants me but then, she glances away and I can see the doubt in the way she bites her lip. I force my voice to not sound too disappointed as I tell her, "Or we can play video games until he leaves."

She sighs. "Video games." She sounds disappointed, but she's definitely not as disappointed as me. But then I remember. Do not take it too far.

Except, as we settle on the floor and she cuddles up to me and we both start hiding from zombies in the game we haven't played in forever, laughing at the way some of them are super walkers, laughing at some of the designs, talking about the TV shows we wished we had time to watch, I know, it's too late.

I'm already way too into her. We've gone too far.

.

CHAPTER 25 - EM

After an hour, Nick turns to me. "You're way too good at this game. Rob taught you how to beat me, didn't he?"

I stick out my tongue. "Maybe. Maybe not. I'll never tell." I laugh, but then sigh as I remember why I'm technically here. Even though the making-out session was more delicious than I could have ever imagined, even though playing video games with Nick is always fun, we need to look through the paperwork, we need to dig in his dad's office.

He stands up. "Come on, we don't have much time. His late afternoon meetings can last anywhere from a few hours to all night."

We shuffle downstairs and push the door to the office. It's locked. "He only locks it before a big case, but he doesn't have a big case right now." He pauses. "Let me ask Sarina if she can open it."

He hurries into the kitchen where Sarina—their maid—is finishing up her work day, and he comes back with a key. "He's going to know we're going into his office because he asked Sarina to tell him if I ever, ever asked for the key."

"Are you sure you want to do this?"

"Even more now than before," he says and turns the key, opens the door. The office is clean—super clean, there are no papers anywhere, but Nick opens shelves and drawers, pulling files out, reading them carefully before putting them back.

"Take the right side, I'll take the left one," he says.

I drag my feet to where he points, feeling uncomfortable looking through his dad's paperwork. "Hey, he's got the picture you made for him in fifth grade." I pick up a drawing in a frame standing on a shelf.

"Probably to show off to whoever comes here that he's a good father," Nick replies.

"Don't be so tough on him. We don't know why he's hiding whatever he's hiding."

"I can't believe you're defending him."

"I'm not. It's just— He's your father, that's all."

"I know," Nick says and continues to storm through the paperwork. I, on the other hand, am very careful with everything I touch. I'm going to need ten hours to go through one drawer.

Nick suddenly screams, "I found it! Of course, he put the file with the personal files, not with the business files." But then he shakes his head as he pulls out some paperwork. "There are only a few pieces of paper. Wait." He focuses on one piece of paper. "There's a birth certificate."

"I have my birth certificate. Mom gave it to me when I started searching. Show me." I cross the room to where he is. I scan through it. It doesn't make any sense. "My birth certificate says my name is Jane Doe. It says I was born as Jane Doe."

Nick pats my arm, pulls me to him, until my head finds its spot in the crook of his neck. "Dad lied to me. He lied to me. My mom's not Jane Doe. She didn't abandon me like he said. My mom really is Claire Carter. And my name's Caroline Carter." Tears I didn't see coming fall down my cheek and I sob. "I don't feel like a Caroline. I'm not Caroline, I'm Emilia."

Nick hugs me tighter. "You are who you want to be. You're my Emilia."

I CRY IN HIS ARMS FOR what seems like forever. I talk to him for what seems like forever, but the time's ticking and I have to get home soon. "I don't want you to be alone," he says. And I almost hope he's going to tell me I can sleep over, but instead he pulls his cell out.

"Rob," he says after a second. "Can you come and pick Em up?" He pauses and frowns. "I haven't done anything. She needs you, man. She needs her brother." He kisses the top of my head and cradles me in his arms. "We're at my place. Okay, we're waiting for you."

He hangs up.

"I don't want to see him," I say and I sound like a whiny five-year-old version of myself.

"You shouldn't be alone right now," Nick repeats. "You're going to want answers, and Rob will be there for you."

"How about you?" I ask and I want to bite my tongue.

"I want to talk to my dad. He can't lie to me with those papers in my hands."

"Thank you," I say. "Thank you for being you."

The doorbell rings only a few minutes later and as soon as Rob sees me, he pulls me into a hug. "What's wrong?" he asks and the tears come back.

"Dad lied. He lied about my adoption. He knows who my mom is."

"What???" Roberto stares at me.

"Dad lied," I repeat.

Roberto shakes his head. "I can't believe it."

"It's true," I say and my tears turn into sob.

Roberto caresses my hair. "Let's go home, let's talk about all this at home." His voice sounds like he's unsure if he should believe me or not, but he's also not letting go of me. He's supporting me. Like he always does.

With his arm around my shoulder, he turns to Nick. "Thanks for taking care of her, man. I owe you one."

"No, you don't. I owe you one if you make sure she gets home safely and that she's okay. Take care of her." Nick sounds serious and they shake hands. It's like they have a new understanding, one I'm not entirely privy to.

"I'll call you tomorrow," Nick tells me and he kisses me. In front of my brother. Like it means something.

If I wasn't so sad, my heart would swell.

Roberto and I head back home and I tell him everything on the way. He sounds too surprised to be in on whatever is going on, and based on what Nick overheard from his parents arguing on the phone, Mom didn't have a clue about Claire Carter.

It leaves Dad.

As soon as we get inside the house, I call his name. I sound drunk, but it's only my pain talking. He stumbles down the stairs, his dark hair sticking everywhere. Not looking like the savvy businessman he usually is.

I blurt much louder than I intended to, "Is Claire Carter my mother?"

Mom follows him downstairs and her eyes widen. "What is she saying? Em, what are you talking about? Your mom abandoned you. We don't know who she is."

My father's shoulders slump. "Yes, your mom is Claire Carter. I paid money for you." He turns to Mom. "I didn't want you to know, Amanda. She was ready to auction off her baby." He bores his eyes into mine. "She was ready to auction you. I couldn't let her do that."

Mom pales and she leans against the wall as if she needed the support. "Why didn't you tell me? Why go through all the trouble to make me believe we went through an agency?" She sounds breathless. We jumped through hoops. We..."

Dad tries to take her hand, but Mom shakes it away from him. His face falls and his shoulders slump. I haven't seen him this defeated even when he lost his job. "You said you didn't want to know who the mother was at the time. And it's complicated."

Mom stares at him. "Tell me now, Dino. Tell us now."

"It was a hard situation. That's all there is to know. Please, trust me, that's all there is to know."

I'm about to ask questions, when Mom beats me to it. "I don't believe you," she says. Her voice rising. "There's more to the story than this. Otherwise, why hide it from me?"

"You would have wanted to go through everything the proper way. You wouldn't have wanted our money to help us the way it did. You would have told me to go to the police." He protests. "You would have done everything right, but that would have meant Em might not be part of our family."

Mom's mouth gapes open and she glances at me, and I want to find a way to reassure her, to tell her I love her, so I simply force my lips into a small smile before turning my full attention back to my father.

"I don't understand," I say. "You bought me. Basically, that's what you're saying. You bought me."

"We saved you," he insists. "No one can say anything about the paperwork. The documents are real. You're our daughter. We played with the rules, we stretched the rules. Some might say we broke the rules. The guy..." He struggles to speak as if the words are too painful. "Your...your birth father didn't know about the adoption at first. And then when he found out, he blackmailed us. Charles helped to take care of everything. The confidentiality agreements, making sure all paperwork was done. We played on the sidelines of the law." He pauses, sighs deeply. "But I don't regret anything." His voice is so sure of himself at this moment, that I'm not certain what to think, how to feel. I still have many questions, so many unanswered questions.

"But Claire was your assistant until eight years ago."

Dad's eyes dart everywhere before settling on a point behind me. "Part of the agreement was to keep Claire working for us for as long as she needed to, as long as she wanted to. She left on her own. Claire is not the one who has loved you all those years."

Tears spring out of my eyes again. "I know that. But why lie to us?"

Mom holds her hand to her mouth, like she's stifling a scream, like there's more to the story than my father is saying. "Yes, why lie to us?" And her voice is too devoid of emotions. Roberto wraps an arm around my shoulder. "Come on, sis, let's get you some hot chocolate with marshmallows." That's the drink Mom used to make me every single time I hurt myself—falling from a bike, feeling rejected by Nick, losing a tooth. "Come on, Mom," Rob says and Mom follows us into the kitchen, leaving Dad behind.

CHAPTER 26 – NICK

I spend several hours with Emilia on the phone. She tells me about the lies, she tells me how she doubts the whole truth came out, she tells me her dad claims he doesn't know where Claire Carter is. She tells me she's not even sure she wants to meet the woman who tried to sell her to the highest bidder.

I continue talking to her, until her words start to slur, until she tells me she's sleepy, until she falls asleep on the phone. My ear is hot from my cell and my body hurts from the position I was in, but I don't fall asleep.

I wait for my father to get home. And he does, at two thirty in the morning.

I sit by his bedroom door and he jumps when he sees me. "What are you doing here?"

I pull out the birth certificate from Em's adoption's file. "We found this."

Dad sits down next to me and I'm pretty sure my mouth has never gaped that wide open. "I knew one day or another you'd find it. I'm surprised you didn't earlier. Sarina called me to let me know you got into the office with Emilia." He pauses. "And, is she happier now than she was before?"

"At least she knows that Claire Carter is her mother."

"Oh, that's what she knows. Interesting." He cracks his knuckles, which in his business suit looks almost ridiculous.

"Where does Claire Carter live?"

"Didn't Dino tell her?"

"He said he has no contact with her," I reply.

"Again, interesting." My father sighs. "I'll help you."

I shake my head, knowing that my father never offers help for free. "And what do I need to do?"

"You need to cool things down with Emilia. And I'm saying that for her sake too. Once you go see Claire Carter, you can be there for her, but as a friend. Otherwise you're going to end up hurting her." He pauses. "Is that what you want? To hurt her even more than she's hurting now?"

"I won't hurt her."

"You will, by going out with Jennifer. As you promised me. And..." He raises a finger to my face. "And...if you forgot this promise, you're going to remember it fast. I'll give you Claire's address today if you promise to go out with Jen, to help me land that business deal by showing everyone how charming you are." He pauses again. "You need to realize, son, that you cannot do all that you please. If I had done that, I'd never be where I am today."

I turn my head to him. He looks tired, worn out and bitter. Is that who I want to be? But then I remember Em's tears, her desire to meet her real mom, and I remember the time and dedication I need to make it as a professional dancer.

I remember my rules. And even though it feels like I'm punching myself in the stomach, I say, "Give me Claire's address."

My father doesn't look like he won an argument; he looks sad as he replies, "You're doing the right thing."

CHAPTER 27 - EM

My eyes must still be red from all the crying I've done yesterday, but I'm trying very hard to stay positive.

Nick called me this morning to tell me he convinced his father to give him Claire Carter's address and phone number.

We know where Claire Carter lives and we're going tomorrow—before I change my mind. We hesitated about contacting her first, but I don't know what to say on the phone, and there's a part of me that's scared she doesn't want to see me. There's a part of me that still doesn't know what to believe. There's a part of me that wants to stop everything and never look back.

But I can't.

I want to ask her what happened back then. I want to ask her why she tried to sell me off. What was going on in her life? I want to make sure she's okay. She did wrap me in the onesie and the blanket. My father told me that when they arranged the pick-up, she had me in those clothes. I want to believe she cared. I want to believe she still cares.

Less than twenty-four hours to go. Nick decided I need to relax somehow so he's taking me to the movies.

I stroll down the street. The sun is warm on my skin but not too hot. It's a perfect summer day and I should enjoy it as such.

The Bam Rose Cinemas in Brooklyn is playing some indie movies, and we'll get to hold hands in the air-conditioned theater.

Nick's waiting for me in front of the theater and I slow my pace to look at him. He's on his phone, probably playing a new game; he's wearing cargo shorts and a Mario Brothers shirt. I'm sure the people around him don't realize that he's not only super hot, he's also on the path to entering a prestigious ballet company. I'm not sure he even realizes how amazing he is.

"You know the best game isn't Mario, it's Zelda," I call and he looks up, grinning as if he hasn't seen me for days, as if he didn't talk to me until I fell asleep on the phone yesterday.

"You are breaking my heart with those words," he jokes and leans down to kiss me on the lips. My heart still flutters at the contact. My heart believes our summer is going to last forever. My heart believes Claire will be happy to see me. My heart believes in happy endings.

My heart is hopeless.

He holds my hand as we pay for our tickets, but right before we enter the theater, a very familiar voice chirps next to us. "Oh my God, Nick! I thought that was you!"

Jen.

A chill runs down my spine. She's ignoring me, of course. Nick squeezes my hand and then lets it go. "I didn't know you were back already."

"I should have called you."

Why? I want to ask her. *So you can try to get back with him? He doesn't want you!* I want to scream.

"Em and I were on our way to watch a movie," he says, nodding my way but not saying or doing anything that would show her we're an item.

Because, we're not.

My heart sinks to my feet and I struggle not to let my pain show in the way I purse my lips.

"Oh Emilia," Jen says with the fakest enthusiasm on the planet. "I didn't see you." *Liar.* She pauses. "Love the dress—even though..." She doesn't finish her sentence, she simply smiles brighter, knowing she managed to rattle me. I'm wearing one my favorite dresses. It's light blue and almost touches my feet, with a thin crisscross on the back.

"I'm so happy to run into you, Nick. Mom says there's a party at your place next week. Love your dad's cocktail parties. They're the best." Nick glances at me, mouthing he didn't know about the party. But it sounds like something his dad would do.

"France was fantastic," she continues to talk. Her black hair looks like silk on her shoulder. Her light brown skin is flawless and she's got dimples when she smiles. She's always very well put together. Today, she's wearing some beige shorts with red ballet flats and a red top that shows off her cleavage. At least I have slightly bigger boobs than she does.

"That's so nice of you to help Roberto out by spending time with his little sister," Jen says, caressing Nick's arm with her index finger.

I'm about to bite it off. She's going to lose a finger; it's not like she needs it to dance.

"You know me. I'm very nice," Nick says. Is he flirting with her? He glances at me and smiles. I'm about to stomp away from both of them, when Jen sighs.

"I have to go. Mom's waiting for me at that little bakery she discovered on this side of town. Apparently, it's better than the caterer she uses on the Upper West Side, but I'll definitely see you guys around. Well, especially you, Nick. We should talk about rehearsing together or maybe go see a show or something."

"We'll talk," Nick replies, and Jen doesn't acknowledge me again as she skips back into the sidewalk, back into her perfect little life. Nick turns to me. "I'm sorry. I know she's a bit much."

"A bit much? She's not the one who seems to be ashamed of me," I reply, grinding my teeth so hard it hurts.

"What?" Nick raises both eyebrows as if what I was saying was some sort of revelation to him, as if he never looked at it that way.

"Come on, you dropped my hand so fast there," I reply, feeling silly because I know what he's going to say. We agreed.

"We agreed," he says. And there we go. An iron fist squeezes my chest but I breathe through it. I'm not going to make a scene here—I did agree to this summer. Only this summer. Technically, it was my idea. My own stupid idea.

"You're right. She gets on my nerves, that's it." That's only half a lie, because right now he also gets on my nerves. For not wanting more. For not even acknowledging the fact he might want more. He wraps his arm around my shoulder and I stiffen instead of relaxing in his embrace.

"Be careful, somebody else might see us," I sneer.

It seems summer is about to end.

CHAPTER 28 - NICK

Em is tense the entire movie, and she's tense on the way back to her place. I can't blame her, but I honestly didn't know how to react when I saw Jen.

I thought Em and I had an understanding, I thought she agreed that it'd be best to not take whatever we're doing past the end of the summer.

And I'm no fucking mind reader. She also gives me mixed signals; she's never said anything about trying to stay together.

I rub the back of my neck and glance at her. She's strolling next to me, but not touching me. Usually our arms would brush, our hands would casually bump into each other and then we'd smile. I love her smile. She's Em.

How can I tell her I agreed to date Jen again to get Claire's address? How can I tell her I've been doing this for two years, dating girls not only because I want to, but to help Dad? How can I tell her my dad would cut all funds to me if he knew we were serious? How can I tell her that I don't think I'm cut out for a relationship? I always put myself first, and my dancing is even more important to me now.

She's blabbering, trying to fill in the silence while we usually never had to. Even our silences were full of unsaid words. Comfortable silences, fun silences, sexy silences. "We're moving next week. I need to start helping Nonna a bit more in the restaurant." She's blushing. The restaurant. Those images of her against the wall, of the way she tentatively touched me, of the way I wanted all of her. How I still want all of her. And I want her to really smile. I'm giving *myself* mixed signals—no wonder she seems confused.

"Em," I say.

She turns to me and her smile isn't the one I'm used to. She's giving me her perfect smile, but there's no warmth in there, only sadness. "Yes?"

"Do you still want me to come with you tomorrow?" My tone is serious and inside, I beg her to say yes.

"Do you want to?" she asks.

I take her hand in mine gently, pulling her away from the traffic on the sidewalk into a little side street, and tilt her head toward mine. There's no way I'm going to let her do this all by herself. I want to be strong for her no matter what she finds. I want to be there for her. "I want to," I tell her.

And then I kiss her.

I wouldn't even care if someone saw.

CHAPTER 29 - EM

Nick parks on the other side of Claire Carter's house. He's stayed silent the entire drive to Jersey, as if he knew I needed time for myself. I played several scenarios in my mind: the hugging one, where all is good and well and she's happy to see me and she bursts into tears apologizing and telling me how much she's missed me and she has a perfect explanation for trying to sell me off, all the way to the I-don't-know-who-you-are scenario where she doesn't even care that I'm here, and the indifferent one.

"Are you sure you don't want me to come with you?" Nick asks, caressing my hand with one finger. It's soothing and comforting and it needs to stop. I can't let myself get even more attached to him. Every moment we've been spending together, I've fallen harder and harder. I've fallen so hard I don't think I'll ever be able to get up again.

"I'm sure. Thanks again for driving," I reply. I didn't want to ask for the car, I didn't want to tell my parents where I was going.

"I'm here. I'm waiting for you right here and if you need anything, you know our sign, right?"

I smile. "I'm not going to moonwalk if I need help. That's ridiculous."

"Whatever." His lips turn into the most heartwarming smile I've ever seen. It's a smile that says "we're good together," it's a smile that says we could stay together, forever. But, what do I know?

Maybe, I'm like all the other ones. Maybe I'm like Jen and I'm only falling for a smile he's used on them.

He leans in and I let myself believe for a second that everything is going to be fine: Nick is going to realize that we can make our relationship work and my birth mother is going to be happy to see me, she's going to invite me inside her house and we're going to have tea.

Why tea?

I don't know...in my mind, it looks like a good way to introduce ourselves.

I kiss Nick gently and then grab the bag I prepared especially for this visit from the backseat and head out to see my mother.

I CAN'T BELIEVE I'M standing here. In front of her home. The streets end in a cul-de-sac with little kids playing with their parents. The houses are big, though not enormous-in-your-face big like Nick's or the one we can no longer afford.

They have nice porches with bunches of roses and welcome signs flowing in the wind.

This is too idyllic, this is too much.

I'm about to ring the doorbell when a kid rushes out the door and bumps into me.

"Sorry, ma'am," he says, and he looks to be about eight years old. He's missing a tooth and wearing a soccer jersey. His curly hair reminds me of mine and my heart stops. Then an older girl follows him outside. She's maybe twelve or something. She has the same locks but her eyes are bright blue and she has better skin than I had at that age. She frowns like she's annoyed at something but then her brother playfully nudges her and she smiles. She has braces and dimples.

They could be my siblings. If for some reason, she and her husband decided not to have me but then had them. I could be looking at my brother and sister or half-brother and half-sister.

"Who are you?" The little boy asks.

My lips form an "o" but no sound comes out. They're staring at me now.

A woman's voice calls from inside. "Wait for me!" And then mutters, "Where did I put my keys again. Shawna, did you see my keys?"

"No!" the girl replies, still looking at me. Even though we don't have the same eye color, I feel like they're similar in a way, maybe in the shape: slightly upturned as Mom would say. She grabs her brother's hand and shields him behind her. Like I'm a threat or something. My stomach crashes like a broken ballerina to my ankles.

The woman—their mother....my mother—steps out, holding a caddy bag with their family name on it. Carter. I'm at the right house. She's less than a foot away from me. The woman who gave birth to me is less than a foot away. I narrow my eyes. Do I look like her? She has a little scar on one cheek—where does it come from? And she's got dimples. I don't. But we have the same smile. At least I think so. Maybe, she remembers me. Granted, she's seen me at least once at that office party. I was only eight then but I'm her daughter, she should have my face imprinted in her memory.

Claire Carter clears her throat with no sign of recognition. "Hi, I'm sorry. We need to run." She pauses. "Are you selling raffle tickets? I've seen other high school students earlier today. I already bought some but maybe if you come back later, you can sell some to my husband." Her voice is warm.

"I'm not," I reply and I hate my voice for breaking, I hate my voice for showing my weakness to her. The little boy pulls on her shirt and she smiles at him.

It's a mother smile, the type of smile that says I love you and I'll always love you, the type of smile that says I can't believe you're a part of me. I've seen that smile before—even though my mother did not give birth to me, she still smiles at me like this. And my heart squeezes so tight I'm afraid I won't remember how to breathe.

Claire Carter—my birth mother—turns to me and then her eyes roam my face. I want her to have a moment of recognition, I want her to understand who I am, but I'm also afraid now of what it would do to her, to her children, to her life.

"Is everything okay?" she asks me.

And I do the only thing I can think of to make her understand without saying the words: my trembling fingers shuffle in my bag and I pull out the little baby blanket she had wrapped me with. The one with the ballerina dancer with a big smile and the words "future ballerina." The one reason why I started dancing so seriously, why I tried out for the School of Performing Arts, why I won't ever give up.

She gasps and takes a step back. She looks at everything but me. Her daughter seems to sense something's wrong because she also pulls on her mom's shirt.

"Mom!" the little boy whines. "I'm going to be late!"

Finally, she looks at me.

For a second.

Nothing more.

Her voice doesn't break like mine when she says, "I have no interest in whatever you're selling. No interest. At all. Don't come back." She squares her shoulders and hurries away from me like being in my mere presence is painful to her. The bag bounces on her shoulder as she pulls her two children with her, ignoring their questions.

She slams the car door behind her and her tires screech as she exits their driveway.

While I'm still standing here.

My broken heart bleeding at my feet.

CHAPTER 30 - NICK

I'm out of the car as soon as I see the woman storm into her Honda. I couldn't hear what she said to Em but it must've been bad, because Em seems to be frozen in place.

"Em!" I call but she doesn't answer. Her body doesn't move. She doesn't turn my way. I'm not even sure she blinks.

"Em," I whisper once I'm close enough to touch her. But she still doesn't say a word. She doesn't cry. She doesn't scream. "Come on, let's go."

I wrap an arm around her shoulder and pull her with me.

"Wait," she says finally. But her tone is dry, there's no emotion. She grabs the blanket that had fallen to the floor. It's dirty but Em holds it close to her heart. She keeps on holding it in the car, the whole drive home, still clutching it as I park in front of her house.

"What happened?" I finally ask.

"There was a scenario I had not considered. That's all. I'll get over it," she replies without looking at me. "I should go." She pauses. "Let's cool it for a while, this thing between us. Summer's not over but people are starting to get back. More people will be at the studio and well, we don't want them to get the wrong idea."

I want to say something. I want to scream that she's wrong. But she's right. If we keep on going, we'll fall into a certain habit. I'm already having a hard time not calling her every single time I feel like talking to someone.

So instead, I don't say anything. I stay silent and she nods her head. Once. "That's what I thought."

And she doesn't even slam the door on her way out.

CHAPTER 31 - EM

My heart hurts so much I don't know what to do with myself. I want to cry. I want to scream. But nothing comes. Nothing. It's like I was a painting in the making and someone erased me. I promised myself that no matter what I found it wouldn't change anything at home, it wouldn't change how I feel, but I can't help but analyze every action, every word.

Are my parents even happy with me? They've got their first child—their blood—accomplishing miracles, helping others, becoming someone. And then they have me—the one they adopted—the one who can't make it to the top, the one who has no idea how to deal with the blow she received right in the stomach.

I bring the blanket to my face, and smell it... I used to believe I could smell my mother's perfume on it, that I could see her tears.

It's all bullshit...

She hates me. I could feel it, the waves of her disdain, of her hate toward me. Like I ruined her. Why?

Why did she even bother with the ballerina blanket if she hated me that much? I don't understand.

Nick's face floats to my mind and bile shoots up in my mouth. He didn't stay. I wanted him to protest when I said we should end it. I wanted him to tell me how much I mean to him. I wanted to hear the words. The ones about love.

But I got nothing.

I grab a pair of scissors from my desk and slice into the fabric of the blanket. I cut it piece by piece, slowly.

Instead of throwing them out though, I carefully place them in my desk drawer, a sad reminder of this day, a sad reminder of what happened.

Mom knocks at my door a couple minutes later. "I'm on my way to help at Nonna's. Since you're already back, do you want to join me?" Her voice is too happy. It doesn't match my mood. Can't she feel that I'm in pieces? Can't she feel that all the hope I had has been torn away from me? Can't she see a hole where my heart used to be?

"No, I'll stay here tonight. I have to watch performances of *Sleeping Beauty's Ballet*. They're thinking about doing it at next year's showcase."

"Don't work too late," she replies without opening the door and skips out, calling Roberto, saying she'll meet him there.

Roberto doesn't even bother passing by my room. I check my phone. No calls. Nothing from Nick. Except his resonating silence in the car, a silence that definitely spoke louder than words.

No words from my so-called friends who are having the time of their lives away from the city. No words from Natalya, who's probably having fun with her best friend, the one she laughs with on the phone from time to time, when she's not consumed by dancing.

Dancing.

That's it. If only I could reach the top. If only I could become number one, then I'm sure it would change. Nick would see me differently. He would be proud to have me by his side. He would be proud to call me his girlfriend. Because let's face it, if he really wanted to, he could date someone. He could have someone. I wouldn't prevent him from training, I would encourage him, I would push him forward. He must know that.

And then my birth mother would also be proud of me; she wouldn't push me away. I could send her an invitation and when she'd see my name, she would beam.

My parents would be proud. I'd accomplish something. Finally, I'd be someone.

Because right now...right now I feel like I'm no one. That no one cares.

I glance around my room and then reach under my bed for the secret box where I keep mementos of Nick. I touch the bracelet he gave me and carefully, I open the drawer where the pieces of what I believed in lie scattered and sad.

CHAPTER 32 - NICK

I hate myself for the pain in her eyes. I punch the wheel and punch it again harder until my knuckles bleed.

But what does it change?

"Your father wanted to let you know that he's expecting you to call Jennifer Harrison today or tomorrow," Sarina tells me as she hands me a glass of fresh water.

I want to throw the glass of water on the family portraits adorning the hallways. But what did Grandmother Madeleine ever do to me?

I climb the stairs and lock the door behind me. I jump on the bed and lie there for what seems for hours. I could go against my father. I could tell him to fuck off. I could explain to him how I feel.

But he would answer that men do not talk about feelings. We're strong. We're here for the win.

I feel like a complete loser right now.

It's almost dark when my cell rings. "Roberto?" I ask. He only calls that late these days if he's had a fight with Giovanni.

"Have you seen Em?"

"Earlier today but it's been a while."

"We can't find her. She's not in her room, she's not at the School, she's not at any of her usual spots." His tone rises. "Where the fuck is she?"

"I think I know."

CHAPTER 33 - EM

I'm out of breath when I arrive at the park. It's almost dark out but there are still groups of people wandering around, five women are jogging and cheering each other on, an old man is sitting on a bench talking to no one in particular.

He seems content to be there. But then, a man about my dad's age sits next to him and they cry together. I don't know what their story is, but my heart cries with them.

The back of my throat hurts and my chest feels heavy.

I hurry away from them, walk until I find our spot. It looks the same and it looks different. That's where I told him I liked him on the Fourth of July. It seems like such a long time ago, it seems like I dreamed this moment, that it never happened.

I imagine him being here, I imagine him leaning closer to me and telling me the words I've been dying to hear. But the fireworks couldn't bring us closer and our relationship isn't meant for the grand gestures, for the grandiose and epic love I always dreamed of.

Nonna told me that my grandfather fought for her, that he courted her for years before her parents even let her talk to him. She laughed, saying they used to sneak out, that it was harder than today without the phone and what she calls the end-of-romance technology. Poppa took her dancing, Poppa told her that he wasn't afraid of going to war but that he was afraid of losing her.

They had a real relationship. They had true love.

What I had with Nick wasn't even a relationship. Just a simple agreement between friends to help each other for the summer.

And the summer is almost over now. Finding my birth mom hasn't changed the face of the world. I only know I need to become better. That I can't be second best anymore.

I take off my shoes and let the grass go through my toes.

"Em!" Nick calls my name, but I don't turn around.

"What are you doing here?" I ask. "How did you even know where to find me?"

"Your brother called me. He was panicked because you weren't home when they got back from your Nonna's restaurant. They all were. They looked for you everywhere. At school, at the usual spots."

I look up at the sky. "I wanted to sleep at school, in the rehearsal room actually, but then I felt the urge to come here, to see the water, to imagine I was on a beach with the warm sand almost burning my feet, with the salt water splattering on my face. So, I came here. Do you remember last year, how much fun we had in the summer?"

He nods and sits behind me, wrapping his arms around me. I stiffen.

"I'm here. I'm here for you," he whispers.

And I don't put up a fight, it doesn't change anything and for a few minutes, I simply want respite. I let myself fall into his embrace because there's nowhere else I'd rather be. "It all seemed easier before. I'm sixteen and I feel like it's never going to be the same again." I pause, but the tears I've been trying to keep inside of me spill out in a sob. "You should have seen the look on her face when I knocked at her door. You should have seen how she closed the door of her car. She didn't close it, she slammed it."

"Maybe she didn't want to be found."

"I'm not sure. It wasn't like she said she didn't want to be found, or it's not like she was scared. She looked disgusted. By me." I shudder, and he tightens his embrace.

There are laughs in the distance and the breeze gets stronger. "She has a family. She has everything she needs. Why didn't she keep me?" My body shivers and my voice trembles. "Why wasn't I enough?"

"Em..." he says, but then I turn my head to him. Our faces are close to one another. I want him to kiss me, I want to feel his lips on mine again. Forget about all those talks we had about not getting involved, forget about all the reasons why it's not a good idea: his career, his parents, my brother, his reputation, my need to focus on dancing...

I'm sixteen and my summer romance cannot end this way. My summer romance cannot end with that hollow feeling inside my chest.

"One last time," I whisper, getting lost in his green eyes.

"One last time," he replies, and his lips find mine.

One last time.

THE END

Do you want to know what happens to Nick & Em? Don't hesitate to check out Always Second Best, <u>available now.</u> Keep on reading to know how to receive exclusive bonus content from A SUMMER LIKE NO OTHER and for a sneak peek of ALWAYS SECOND BEST.

A little message to my readers

Dear Reader,
      Thank you SO MUCH for reading A SUMMER LIKE NO OTHER! I know you have the choice between a lot lot loooot of books and I'm grateful you took a chance on mine.

Hope you enjoyed getting to know Emilia & Nick!

If you have a few minutes, it'd be awesome if you leave just three words as a review for this book. Reviews really help authors. If you do leave a review and also would like to receive the following **extra exclusive bonus scenes** (just email me at: authorelodienowodazkij@gmail.com)

- Emilia and Nick flirting in the Hamptons.
- The last scene of this book from Nick's POV

You don't have to leave a review to receive this bonus content (but I would be very grateful if you did), you can also receive those scenes by signing up for my newsletter.[1] You can of course do both ☺

---

1.   https://mailchi.mp/elodienowodazkij/aslno

And if you'd like to follow me on social media, I am on Instagram[2], Twitter[3] and Facebook[4]. You can also follow me on BookBub.[5]

I do share pictures of Plato The Dog and Bobbie Voltaire the Cat quite often.

Thank you again so very much for reading!

And don't forget ALWAYS SECOND BEST is available now. Keep on reading for a sneak peek. ☺

<3

2.　　https://www.instagram.com/enowodazkij/

3.　　https://twitter.com/ENowodazkij

4.　　https://www.facebook.com/enowodazkij

5.　　https://www.bookbub.com/profile/elodie-nowodazkij

SNEAK PEEK

CHAPTER 1 – EM

I SHOULD HAVE STAYED at the School of Performing Arts this weekend. I should have spent more time rehearsing for our big end-of-the-year showcase audition. I should have repeated each movement until I reached perfection...

I'm never going to be ready.

My throat tightens. I need more hours, more days, more time.

"Do you want more lasagna?" my grandmother—Nonna—asks. Her gray hair is cut short and even though the lines on her face are getting more pronounced, even though she's pale and thinner, even though she gets tired more easily, her smile is still the brightest in all of New York. "Or maybe more salad?" She mixes the tomato mozzarella salad again. She grows the basil herself, and believes that she could have an entire menu using only recipes with basil, like pesto steaks, or basil sorbet.

"A bit more salad, please." I hand her my plate. Nonna's restaurant is usually bright and full of laughter and people and waiters trying not to run into one another, but tonight it's only her and me. Nonna opens the restaurant for lunch on Sundays and keeps her evening free.

"There you go." She sips her water. "Your father was so cute when he was little. That day he brought me a bouquet with roses from our garden, I didn't have the heart to tell him he shouldn't have cut them. Instead, I made sure to put one in his baby book," she says and then inhales deeply as if trying to catch her breath. She smooths the red tablecloth on our small table. She called tonight a "grandmother-granddaughter" date night, setting up candles and even putting some Italian music on in the background.

Even though I should be rehearsing, I couldn't say no to her. I didn't want to say no. And not because her lasagna is the best in town.

"I'm talking, I'm talking but I know you have to go," she says, standing up, holding on to her chair.

"I can stay," I reply.

"You're sweet, but you've started to fidget on your chair, that means you're already running late."

I cringe—I hadn't noticed I was doing that. "Dinner was really delicious. Thank you." I gather the plates, but she takes them away from me.

"I'll take care of that. You go."

And there's so much tenderness in the way she looks at me that I want to bottle up the emotion I feel and keep it for when I have a bad day, or for when I see Nick—my forever crush, my brother's best friend, the guy who broke my heart last summer. I hold her arm and together we walk to the entrance. The restaurant smells of fresh bread mixed with garlic and basil. It smells of my childhood spent in the kitchen with her and Poppa.

When everything was so much easier.

I grab my coat, careful not to knock one of the pictures she has on the walls. Her memory wall, as she calls it. Lots of pictures of Poppa, and my own father, and my entire family, and of Italy. She recently put one up of Mr. Edwards, the man who has been courting her for almost a year now.

"Goodbye, Bellissima," she says, kissing my cheeks loudly. "Thanks for spending time with your old grandmother." She winks.

"You're not old."

"You're right. I'm ancient." She laughs and hugs me again. The perfume Mom gets her every Christmas is another reminder of all the happy times I've had with her. She coughs and leans against the wall. "I know you wanted to stay at school this weekend, so thank you again." And before I can reply, she pushes me out the door. "Now, go. You don't want to be late."

"Love you," I tell her. I put on my coat and my scarf.

"I love you too, Bellissima." She pauses. "And say hi to Nicholas for me," she says.

Nicholas. Nick. I force my lips into a smile, I force myself to not think about Nick. I force myself to wave to Nonna. "I'll see you next week."

And I glance at her one more time before slowly making my way to the subway. I used to love going back to school on Sundays. I used to wait for Nick at the corner of our street and we'd walk together. We'd talk about our weekend. He'd make me laugh and I'd try to not stare at his lips while he talked about his parents, our last audition, the video game he managed to get his hands on before its release, because he knew I wanted to play it and he knew some guy who could make it happen.

That was before.

Now, I take the subway from Brooklyn, where my family and I moved after Nick's father fired my dad.

Alone.

Now, I don't spend every possible second with Nick, I don't send him random text messages to make him laugh, I don't smile every time I see him.

Now, I avoid him as much as possible and lie to his face about dating some guy I met at my Nonna's restaurant.

I readjust my bag on my shoulder and look up at the gray sky. New York has had its share of snow and winter and icy sidewalks but it seems we're in for another round, even though we're already in March. There's a small coffee shop nestled between bigger buildings one block before the subway. It's crowded and I'm tempted to push the door and get in line. Hide in there and forget about real life. Forget about school.

But instead of entering the coffee shop, I march straight ahead. I pass a group of students who are talking about an epic party they went to yesterday, and I barely avoid a couple whose PDA is so over the top I can almost hear my brother telling them to get a room. I settle in an empty seat in the subway.

And my mind wanders to the same game it always plays. If the third person to enter the car is a woman, I'm going to talk to Nick. Really talk to him. I'll come clean about not seeing anyone.

The first person who enters the subway is a woman with hair to her shoulders and a big smile that shows a gap in her middle teeth, and she's holding the hand of another woman with dark hair, who's the second person to enter the car. She gives her girlfriend a kiss on the lips, before whispering something into her ear. They both start giggling. The third person to enter the car is a guy. The guy's not wearing a coat despite the freezing temperatures. His Hugo Boss shirt is tight around his muscles and his jeans must cost more than an entire semester at the School of Performing Arts. Based on the price of his outfit, he's not jacketless because he can't afford one; it's a fashion statement. A fashion statement that could freeze him to death.

Maybe I could count the couple as only one person and if the next passenger is a woman, then I would talk to Nick. A group of guys enter the subway.

I sink into my seat.

The universe has spoken—I won't talk to Nick today.

My phone vibrates in my back pocket and I slide it out. A text from my brother—not Nick.

Sorry I couldn't make it home this weekend, this experiment is killing me. Literally, it could kill me. Playing with virus is dangerous.

I crack a smile. Roberto can be a tad dramatic, but he's also a genius in physics and medicine and whatever else he touches. He's going to graduate from college two years early and save the world.

I type back: *Be careful.*

Always

I settle into my seat again, trying very hard to not remember what Roberto told me about the amount of viruses and bacteria and all that jazz crowding public transportation. A guy sitting two benches down is eating chicken tenders, and the scent surrounds me. I'm not hungry—not after eating lasagna with Nonna, but the smell reminds me of carefree evenings on the rooftop of Nick's house two years ago during Thanksgiving break. That's when our families still got along, and that's when we decided we didn't want to simply sit at their fancy table with their fancy meals and their fancy friends. We ordered KFC and climbed on the roof and talked all night. The three of us: Roberto, Nick and me.

A little girl with straight black hair and eyes slanting upwards enters the car with her mom. She has a big smile on her face and points to the seat in front of me. "Can we sit, Mommy?" Her mom nods.

They sit in front of me and the little girl snuggles up to her mom. Their purple jackets look similar with a snowman on the front pocket. The girl glances around and then she stands up to touch my bag.

"Lola," her mom calls and she sits back down, still staring at my bag.

Her face lights up and her grin turns wider. She reminds me of the kids on the poster for the Buddy Walk that was organized two weeks ago in the city to raise awareness about Down syndrome.

"Are you a ballerina?" she asks slowly with a laugh in her voice, her finger pointing to the pictures on my bag: ballet pointes and a dancer in a tutu.

"Yes, I am," I reply—trying to ignore the feeling in my gut that comes with the words. I don't know what it is, but it's unwelcome. I miss the joy that used to light my chest when I'd speak about dancing.

"I have Down syndrome," she says—very matter-of-fact, and before I can react she continues, "But I'm going to be a basketball player." Her mom kisses the top of her head.

"She's an amazing basketball player already." The mom winks. "But she also wants to be an ice skater and a lacrosse player and a gymnast, depending on what she sees on TV." She laughs. And a smile dances on my lips. They look so happy.

"I'm sure you'll be great," I tell her. She nods firmly as I wave goodbye. "This is my stop."

She waves back at me. "You're going to be great too!" And her vote of confidence means more to me than the latest "you can do it" speech I got from one of my teachers. Maybe because she seemed to believe it, while my teacher had a pity look on her face, the one that says, "I'm obligated to give you a pep talk, but in reality, you kind of suck."

The auditions are in three days. Three. Days.

I know I can do it. I know I have what it takes.

Note to self: work harder.

CHAPTER 2 - NICK

THE HOUSE SMELLS LIKE the apple pie our cook made for dinner last night: caramel and cinnamon. I think he took pity on me since our planned family dinner turned into a "Nick eats alone and plays video games all night" type of dinner. He knows apple pie with meringue is one of my favorite desserts. My true favorite dessert is the one Em made this summer: cannoli. Right before we started making out. She still had the taste of the Italian dessert on her lips.

I should remember not to think about Em, or about the way her kisses put fire in my veins, or about the way she felt in my arms. Because getting hard at my parents' house when they're only a few feet away is so not the way I want to end my weekend.

I shift on my feet and grab my bag, ready to head out without so much as a goodbye. I guess I'm still pissy after they ditched me yesterday. Most of my friends rave about the time they get to spend away from their parents, but that's much different when the time you get to spend with them is the exception to the rule. I wouldn't mind a few awkward dinners, a few questions about the school, my life. Something.

"You're already leaving?" Mom pops out of the living room, where she was on the phone for some fundraiser she's organizing in two months. She's not as sad as she used to be, but she's still not entirely present when she's home. The therapy sessions they drag me to at least once a month have helped, but it's like she focuses so much on mending her relationship with Daddy Dearest that she's not sure how to handle me. There are times when she reaches out to me, carves time in her busy schedule to talk to me and other times, when we barely see each other on weekends.

"It's late," I reply and rub the back of my neck. I'm much taller than her, but when she's looking at me a certain way, I revert back to my five-year-old self who didn't want to stray far from her. Back to when I believed my parents were heroes. I want to laugh at past-me and tell present-me to get a grip.

"I'm sorry we were so busy this weekend, but I promise next week, you and I will do something fun together."

"Okay." I don't hold my breath.

"How is Emilia doing these days?" she asks, narrowing her eyes at me like she's trying to read through my usual bullshit.

"She's doing well." I keep my tone as light as possible; even hearing Emilia's name feels like someone's punching me right in the chest. I fucked it all up and I don't know how to make it right. If I had a normal relationship with Mom, if Dad wasn't all set on me not dating Em, maybe I could ask her for advice. Em says she's seeing someone. I don't believe her...not because I think I'm irreplaceable but because she doesn't look happy. If she had moved on, she'd be happy. Right?

"I'm glad to hear that," she replies, touching a vase she received from the former governor of New York's wife, rearranging it slightly so it's perfectly in the middle of the small pedestal. I clench my fists. And it's my turn to really look at her: her lips are pursed as if she wants to say something else but doesn't while her hands are shaking a little, and they only shake when she's worried about something

"I...." My voice croaks like a thirteen-year-old boy's.

Her fingers trace the pattern of the vase—a blue flower. "We haven't seen her in a very long time," she says. I clench my fists harder, exhale loudly, trying to lift the pressure on my chest. Mom's doing better, and I don't want to push her away, to hamper her recovery, *our* recovery, by asking what's on the tip of my tongue. *Did you know?* My mind screams, begs her to read my thoughts. *Did you know Dad blackmailed me into dumping Emilia and dating other people—especially daughters of his buddies—to win a business deal?*

She tilts her head to the side. "We haven't seen Roberto in a long time either."

"They're busy. Everyone's busy." My tone is a bit more biting than intended. "Anyways, I have to go, but I'll be back next Friday night or Saturday." I force my lips into a short smile. The anger building up inside of me like a crescendo doesn't have much to do with Mom—it's more about me being a coward.

Every week, I tell myself I'm going to have the balls to confront Daddy Dearest. Every week, I brace myself to tell him I will no longer do as he tells me, that I won't give in to his blackmailing. No more dating girls because he says so. Every week, I fail. Either he's not home, or he's with Mom and she shouldn't become collateral damage. She seems so fragile at times, so ready to simply leave us behind and never look back.

Her phone rings and she raises a finger. "Wait a second," she tells me before picking up. Something about the fundraiser again. She puts her *nothing is wrong* mask on; her voice is stronger, but it's not happy. I'm pretty sure none of her so-called *luncheon friends* know about her problems.

My parents drag me to therapy "for the greater good of our family." I usually grunt a lot on the way there, but it's not all that bad. Mom apologized for leaving me behind when she needed time to think. She told me it wasn't about me, but it sure as hell felt that way when she packed up her bags and went on spa-cation for three months. I drove all the way to see her for her birthday, with Em holding my hand. Mine was early October and she didn't even call me. I told her that. She cried and my throat tightened so much I didn't think I was ever going to be able to breathe normally again.

"What do you want, Nicholas?" the therapist—Dr. Grahams—asked me during a grueling one-on-one session we all had to take before our family hour. I didn't answer, and he scribbled on his notepad. "Your desire to be accepted by your father should not overshadow your own needs, your own person," he said, and asked me to keep that in mind.

I'm trying to.

"Of course, Laura. You'll be the first to know," Mom says and rolls her eyes at the same time. "Listen, I have to go. Nick is about to leave for school."

I stare at her and then shift my bag to my other shoulder.

I don't want to ask Mom if she knows about Dad's blackmailing. Believing she didn't know is much easier. I need to believe one of my parents is not out there to use me.

She hangs up. "Tell Emilia hello from me," she says and I wince.

Way to sucker-punch me without knowing it, Mom.

"Sure thing," I reply. I've told Em I was sorry about how we ended things last summer. But I've never told her why. I've never told her how much I wish things were different. How much I want her back.

The therapist also told us of the importance of making amends, of how the truth would set us free.

Yeah, right.

Asking Mom if she knows about the blackmail gives me more jitters than the auditions coming up. But telling Em? Managing to do a butterfly—lifting myself off the floor as high as possible, twisting my body and landing gracefully on one knee—is nothing compared to spilling out the truth.

I can take the hate in her eyes, but not the hurt and the disgust.

Mom air-kisses me, landing a hand on my shoulder. She's definitely a bit more touchy-feely since we started therapy. "I know you've got a busy week coming with the auditions. And I know you wish your father would be more supportive."

"Understatement of the year." I drop my bag to the floor and cross my arms over my chest. *You're being defensive,* our therapist would say. I hesitate between mentally giving him the finger for intruding on my thoughts or shrugging because he's right.

"He's learning. He's doing better already."

True. Even with me, he's doing better. He hasn't asked me to date anyone for his business for the past three months. He's been much more careful around me, and he's been much more silent too, less pushy, less annoying, less everything. Definitely not more supportive, but not as destructive.

"You'll see. It's going to be a great year for you. For us. For our family." She touches my shoulder again. It's awkward but it's there.

"Okay, Mom. See you next week." And I do something I haven't done in such a long time. I bend down and press my lips to her cheek. "Love you, Mom."

Her hand flies to her face and her smile isn't fake. "Love you too, Son."

I can't remember the last time she's said it. I almost try to make a joke about it, anything to deflect the hope building inside of me, anything to not get hurt in the future if all goes down to shit again. But then I look at her and how she's trying, how she's opening up, how she's working hard on herself.

My lips turn up into a smile. Not the "I'm happy to leave this place" smile that I usually have when I go back to school.

This time it's a real, no-afterthought smile.

CHAPTER 3 - EM

LEAVING THE STUFFY subway behind, I climb the stairs to the Central Park exit. The cold air engulfs me. I tighten my scarf and put on my winter hat—Nick has the same one. They have our respective names on them. Nonna gave them to us for Christmas a few months ago, and talk about awkward around the tree when Nick opened his. He was there because his parents were in couples' therapy and Roberto begged Dad to let Nick spend Christmas with us. Dad wouldn't have agreed if Mom didn't plead his case.

I pretended to have a date on Christmas day with a mystery guy to avoid him. I pretended to have moved on. I pretended my heart didn't hurt seeing him sad.

I've done a lot of pretending since last summer.

I push the door of the School of Performing Arts. "Good evening," I tell the young receptionist who's working the weekend shift. She glances up from her magazine and waves—she's been there since February, apparently paying her way through grad school at NYU. The spotless entrance and the posters and brochures give way to narrow hallways. I turn to get into my dorm room. Some students go home on weekends, especially if, like me, their families live close by, but my roommate, Natalya, hasn't been home in a few months. She's supposed to fly back to Maine right after the auditions.

"Hey," I tell her as I enter our small room and carefully place my bag on the chair by my desk. The standard dorm room doesn't allow for much distraction: no TV, bunk beds, two desks and one big closet. And as usual, Nata's side is full of stuff while mine is spotless. Nata is glancing through pictures, her iPod buds in her ears. She takes them out and smiles.

"Hi. How was your weekend?" She puts up her long blonde hair in a messy ponytail that looks amazing on her.

"My weekend was good. I wanted to come back earlier to rehearse though, but didn't want to leave my Nonna."

"I get it. I wish I could have spent more time with my babushka." Nata's voice is sad and I want to kick myself in the butt for reminding her about her loss. Her grandmother passed away in January and it was a very tough time for her.

My mind fills with pictures of Nonna—laughing, hugging me, telling me she believes in me—and I hold on to those pictures, pushing away the way she looked on her hospital bed after her stroke last January: small, so small. And so fragile. I busy my hands with emptying my bag from the weekend and putting my dirty clothes in the hamper. I should have done my laundry at home, but spending time with Nonna was more important.

"Do you want to go grab something to eat at the cafeteria?" Nata asks. I sometimes bring her food from Nonna's restaurant, but she's super careful with what she eats. I should be too.

"No, thanks. I've got a few things to do," I reply, pointing to my laptop. "Got to make sure I ace some of the classes, in case I don't get a part in the showcase."

"You're going to get one, and an amazing one," Nata says. She doesn't say the best one because, well, when you're competing for the number one spot, you only wish it for yourself. "Do you want me to bring you anything?"

"I'm fine. I ate lasagna before coming back, but thanks."

"Sure. I won't be long." She glances behind her shoulder. "I'll pick up the mess when I get back, promise."

My lips turn up into my *I don't believe you but it's okay* smile and I reply, "Yeah, yeah. Whatever."

"I promise I will. I had to rehearse a lot this weekend. I couldn't get myself high enough in the air for a simple *grand jeté*." She sighs. "No matter how many times I tried, my body wouldn't cooperate."

"I'm sure you managed at the end."

"It was okay, but not perfect." She smiles slightly. "Yet." She closes the door behind her. Nata's not only gorgeous, she's also well on her way to becoming the first junior ever to get the main role in a showcase.

I pick up one of her books and put it on her nightstand, sliding the picture of her and her best friend a bit to the side. They're jumping into a lake, laughing and holding hands.

At school she's so much more reserved. Some students think she's shy, others believe she's full of herself because she's gorgeous and talented—with her blonde hair falling down past her shoulders, her blue eyes, the way she lights up the scene as soon as she steps into it—but most either want to be her or be with her. Nata and I have been roommates for three years, and she's one of my only friends here—but even I don't really know what's been going on and why she's been looking down.

I sit back at my desk. Maybe I should have gone with Nata to the canteen to keep her company, but another reason we've been pretty good roommates is that we give each other some space.

I inhale deeply, count to three and click on a document entitled "Letter – Fourth draft." I've been working on it for three weeks, and it's still not ready. I need to get every word right, and that has nothing to do with any school assignments.

It's a letter for my birth mother.

Dear Claire,

I hope it's okay I call you Claire. My name's Emilia, that's the name my parents gave me. I'm not sure why I'm writing this letter.

I'm not sure if you'll even read it, but I want to tell you a story. A story about me and maybe, you'll decide that you do want to meet me after all.

I simply want to understand.

I erase "I simply want to understand." I delete the first lines. I don't need to tell her my name. She knows me, she knows my name. She knows my entire family. She used to be my father's secretary, after all.

I reread all the words out loud. Slowly. My voice sounds way too mechanic, too detached, and the words don't compute. They're not enough. They don't explain the void I've felt inside ever since she slammed her door in my face.

When I thought about finding my birth mother, our imaginary reunion was full of smiling and hugging and talking and laughing.

Instead, my heart exploded in a thousand pieces that I don't think I'll ever manage to tape back together. I don't think she could have run away from me faster than she did when I tried to talk to her last summer, and if she'd slammed the door of her car any harder, it would have been destroyed.

Like my feelings.

I tap my fingers on the desk, get up, sit back down, stare at the screen.

The memories of last summer scream in my ears. How Dad got tired of my digging around, of me asking questions. How my heart dropped at my feet and took forever to find its place in my chest again when he finally told me the truth. That my birth mother wanted to sell me to the highest bidder, how he bought me from her, how he'd been lying to me all those years.

I minimize the window and go into the folder I named "Truth folder."

Over the summer, we—Nick and me—found next to nothing about Claire, but it's amazing what a bit of money can do. So many sites gather information on people. And it doesn't hurt that I found her social security number in Dad's old office paperwork.

I reread the file. Her parents died in a car accident when she was young. She pulled herself and her little sister through college. She worked several jobs then, but after college seemed to be doing pretty well for herself.

The loud buzz of my alarm startles me, reminding me I need to do some stretching exercises. I close the document, then the folder. My finger hovers for two seconds before closing the letter without even saving it. Sending this letter would be stupid, ridiculous, desperate. I need one that might convince her talking to me is a must.

My alarm rings again and I reach out for my phone. It's almost eight p.m.—Nata's going to be back soon. Nick should be in his room now. Unless he's out with another girl. Yet again.

The churning in my stomach hasn't receded; it's still as strong as the first time I saw him after breaking things off last summer.

I was running late. For the first time ever. I turned in the hallways to make it to our first school assembly meeting of the year and there he was leaning against the wall, Jen snuggling against him. I muffled a scream and fought back tears.

Two weeks before, his lips were on mine, his arms were around my waist, his fingers were trailing up and down my back.

They weren't kissing, but it was clear they were back together. I had heard the rumors, I had seen tweets, but I didn't want to believe it. We had agreed we would only have one summer together: one summer that was supposed to be easy. After all, the terms were simple: he didn't want to have a relationship once school started because he wanted to concentrate on his career, plus with our parents not getting along and my brother breathing down our neck, it made sense to keep it limited.

I was not supposed to fall even more in love with him, I was not supposed to get my heart broken. I was not supposed to hope we would forget about the expiration date on our relationship and keep going.

But when everything went crashing faster than a dancer missing his or her landing, I still had hope. I dreamed that he'd come and knock at my door, that he'd tell me he was sorry, that he'd fight for me.

Note to self: stop being delusional.

"Hi!" Jen had called my name and waved with the biggest and most triumphant smile on her face.

Nick opened his mouth but he didn't say a word.

We stared at each other. I thought I saw regret in his eyes, but most likely he was only squinting to figure out if I was mad or not. I swallowed my pain and my pride, and I waved at them. Like it didn't slice my heart in two to see them together.

Whatever. It's been eight months. I'm over it. And even if I wasn't over it, I wouldn't let myself get hurt like this again.

The only way for me to come out of all this on top is to get the starring role at this year's showcase. I have the scenario in my head. I get the main part and I send another letter to my birth mother; she's so proud she comes to see me. I get the main part and Nick finally realizes we're right for one another. I get the main part and my parents look at me with as much pride as when Roberto told them he won a scholarship to spend a summer at MIT next year.

I stare at the dark computer screen.

I see my future. I see what I want, what I need.

I get up. My muscles tense and flex with determination.

This main part is mine.

ALWAYS SECOND BEST IS AVAILABLE NOW!

ACKNOWLEDGEMENTS

Wait. What? Did I write and revise and revise and revise and publish my third book? Wow! I can't believe it! <3 This book came to me as I was drafting ALWAYS SECOND BEST, which also follows Nick & Em, but with a lot of struggles. The reason I was struggling was because I knew this summer had happened between them, but I couldn't picture how it affected them, how it had such an impact on their relationship. So, I started drafting their summer and ten pages turned into twenty, into thirty, into more than a hundred, and it was a story that I fell in love with. A story that I wanted to share because I wanted you all to meet Em & Nick during that summer, and I really cross my fingers you fell in love with them—at least a little bit.

As always, a book—even a novella—is the work of dozens of people. Without them, I wouldn't be able to write and publish. Like my copy editor Stephanie Parent ☺, who helps make my words shine.

And, I am so thankful to so many people who make this writing journey unbelievable.

I am so so so so so grateful for all the readers, bloggers, reviewers who take a chance on my books. I really cross my fingers you fall in love with Em & Nick the way I did.

My husband—the Chemical Engineer—always sees a part of himself in the love interests (he's totally right by the way), and believes in me, believes that I will make a living writing, and he enables me to do what I love. I don't know what I can do to thank you! Well, okay, I'll get you more Magnum ice creams at the store. <3

My family who is far but oh so close. I know I don't get to see you often, but I know you have my back and I know that you believe in me too, and it means the world. And yes, I promise my books will be translated in French and German soon.

My writer friends, you know, the ones I turn to when I need my hand to be held or a gentle kick in my writing butt. You know who you are (I'm not naming anybody here because I am so afraid to forget someone it hurts).

Riley Edgewood and Katy Upperman, thank you for the chains of emails. Without your encouraging words, Nick and Em might not be real as they are today.

Tracey Neithercott, Alison Miller and Riley Edgewood, thank you for helping my blurb shine. It was nowhere near as good as it is now when it was just me fiddling with it—you made it what it is today.

Riley and Alison, I bake you all the cookies and give you all the wine and Riley, all the brie, for sending me such amazing feedback. Nick and Em wouldn't be who they are without you. Your comments reassured me and pushed me to not only dig deeper, but also to make sure I didn't cut any corners. And thanks to you, there's also more kissing in the book. And I heart you.

To the #RSWrite ladies (Jaime Morrow, Erin Funk, Katy Upperman, Alison Miller), this writing intensive always helps me stay focused and in this case, helped me finish my book. Annnnnd to the ladies in the magic spreadsheet, the one that makes words come true, thank you for your encouraging words and the occasional kick in the butt as I was drafting A SUMMER LIKE NO OTHER: Riley Edgewood, Lola Sharp, Tracey Neithercott, Jessica Love, Elizabeth Briggs, Jaime Morrow, Katy Upperman, Ghenet Myrthil.

To all my friends, near and far, thank you! Thank you for understanding when I'm holed up writing or revising. Thank you for your support and for everything.

More books by the author

Broken Dream series
ONE DREAM ONLY (Natalya's prequel #0.5)
ONE, TWO, THREE (Natalya's story)
A SUMMER LIKE NO OTHER (Em & Nick #1)
ALWAYS SECOND BEST (Em & Nick #2)
LOVE IN B MINOR (Jen's story)
Gavert City series
FEAR ME, FEAR ME NOT (Erin & Dimitri)
SEE ME, SEE ME NOT (Tessa & Luke)
TRUST ME, TRUST ME NOT (Lacey & Hunter)
Available as audiobook:
ONE DREAM ONLY
ONE, TWO, THREE
A SUMMER LIKE NO OTHER
LOVE IN B MINOR
FEAR ME, FEAR ME NOT

About The Author

ELODIE NOWODAZKIJ WAS raised in a tiny village in France, where she could always be found a book in hand. At nineteen, she moved to the US, where she learned she'd never lose her French accent. Now she lives in Maryland with her husband, their dog and their cat.

She's also a serial smiley user.

Visit Elodie online at:

www.elodienowodazkij.com

www.facebook.com/enowodazkij

twitter.com/ENowodazkij

instagram.com/ENowodazkij

Made in the USA
Middletown, DE
08 December 2020